TOEIC L&R TEST
多益閱讀解密

Katsuno Shibayama
Robert Hilke
Paul Wadden, Ph.D.
／著

許可欣、黃薇嬪
／譯

Reading

眾文圖書 股份有限公司

前言

「TOEIC L&R TEST 多益解密系列」是專為第一次參加 TOEIC 測驗的考生所編寫，全系列包括《TOEIC L&R TEST 多益聽力解密》、《TOEIC L&R TEST 多益文法解密》以及《TOEIC L&R TEST 多益閱讀解密》。此系列所設定的目標分數為 600 ～ 800 分，特別適合一般企業求職者（600 分）、公司外派人員（700 分）以及高階主管（800 分）的英語要求。

「TOEIC 的閱讀測驗好難，而且時間不夠寫不完，怎麼辦才好？」這是考生常有的心聲。為幫助考生有效提高閱讀測驗的成績，筆者親自上場應試，分析實際考題，找出各類型文章的規則，並根據研究成果編寫出與正式測驗內容相仿的模擬試題，隨著新制 TOEIC 登場，筆者更進一步配合新的測驗形式，更新內容而完成《TOEIC L&R TEST 多益閱讀解密》一書。

新制 TOEIC 的閱讀測驗增加了「語意理解題」、「句子填空題」和「三篇文章測驗」，不少考生因為不習慣而感到不安。但是各位請放心，不論是語意理解題、句子填空題或三篇文章測驗，都是有規則可循的。

本書將帶你用三個步驟破解 TOEIC L&R TEST 的閱讀測驗：

1. 看懂不同文章的格式，記住各類文章的閱讀重點。
2. 記住常見題目及正確答案在文中的表達方式。
3. 做練習題。

最後再挑戰一回完整的 TOEIC L&R TEST 的閱讀測驗，測測自己的實力。只要按照本書的步驟循序漸進學習，你一定能夠提高 TOEIC L&R TEST 的成績。

Katsuno Shibayama
Robert Hilke
Paul Wadden

✴ TOEIC L&R TEST 簡介

TOEIC L&R TEST 是由 ETS（Educational Testing Service，美國教育測驗服務社）所研發的一項英語能力測驗，用來評估英語非母語者的商務英文溝通能力，目前已發展成為一項國際性的英語能力認證考試。

TOEIC L&R TEST 是指 Listening & Reading（聽力與閱讀）測驗，另有 TOEIC SW TEST，提供考生評量口說與寫作能力，考生可自行選擇是否加考這部分測驗。

TOEIC Part 1 ∼ Part 7 題型介紹

TOEIC 測驗分為 Part 1 ∼ Part 7 共七部分，Part 1 ∼ Part 4 為聽力測驗，Part 5 ∼ Part 7 為閱讀測驗。

✴ 聽力測驗（100 題，約 45 分鐘）

Part	題數	測驗說明
1 照片描述	6	根據試題冊上的照片，聆聽播放的四個選項，選出一個最符合照片情境的描述。選項不會印在試題冊上。
2 應答問題	25	聆聽播放的題目及三個答案選項，選出最符合題目的選項。題目及選項都不會印在試題冊上。
3 簡短對話	39	聆聽播放的兩人或三人對話，回答試題冊上的題目。每段對話有三個題目，其中有三段對話需要搭配試題冊上的圖表作答。
4 簡短獨白	30	聆聽一段人物發言、廣播、新聞報導或電話留言，回答試題冊上的題目。每段獨白有三個題目，其中有兩段獨白需要搭配試題冊上的圖表作答。

＊閱讀測驗（100 題，75 分鐘）

Part	題數	測驗說明
5 單句填空	30	閱讀一句英文句子，句中有一處空格，從四個答案選項中，選出一個最適合填入空格的選項，以完成一個完整的句子。
6 短文填空	16	閱讀一篇短文，內容可能是一封電子郵件、一份說明書或一篇廣告，其中會有四個空格，須從四個答案選項中，選出一個最適合填入空格的字彙、片語或句子。共有四篇短文。
7 閱讀測驗	54	包括單篇文章測驗（29 題）、雙篇文章測驗（10 題）及三篇文章測驗（15 題）。單篇文章為每一篇文章搭配二～四個題目；雙篇文章為每兩篇搭配五個題目；三篇文章為每三篇搭配五個題目。文章取自即時通訊訊息、報紙或雜誌的短篇報導、廣告、公告或商業文件等。

TOEIC 報考資訊

有關 TOEIC 考試日期、報名方式或申請證書等相關資訊，可以上 TOEIC 台灣官方網站 (http://www.toeic.com.tw) 查詢。

✲ 本書特色與使用方法

學習步驟

為幫助學習者徹底掌握每一個文章類型的閱讀重點和解題方式，本書以下列方式編排：

$\boxed{\text{Introduction}}$ 先看 Part 7 應考對策

本書架構

◆ Day 1-9 閱讀重點與常見題目

● Step 1 閱讀重點
每天學習一種文章類型的閱讀重點。

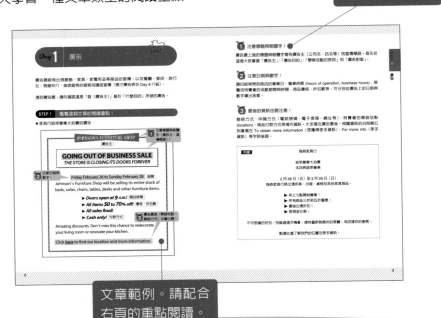

● Step 2 常見題目

熟悉常見題目，以及正確答案在文中的表達方式。

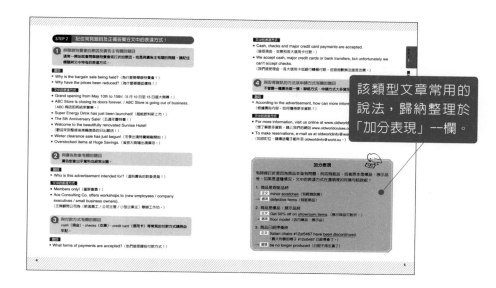

● 練習題

學會如何抓到閱讀重點，並熟悉常見題目後，再透過「練習題」進一步練習。

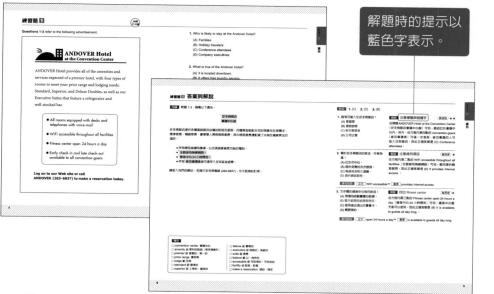

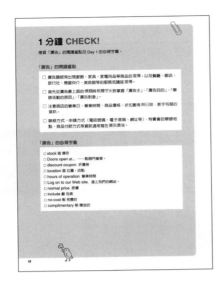

● **1 分鐘 CHECK!**
每日學習內容的總整理。看看你是否都
記住了。

◆ **Day 10 模擬測驗**
收錄一回完整 Part 7 模擬試題，題數與實際測驗相同。

◆ **重要字彙一覽表**
歸納 Part 7 必須記住的字彙。

5 大對策 CHECK!

- ☑ **1 注意時間分配**
  （目標是 1 題 1 分鐘快讀快答）
- ☑ **2 學會解題順序**
- ☑ **3 了解常見題目形式**
- ☑ **4 分辨文章類型，快速找出正確答案**
- ☑ **5 依據文章類型，找出該類型固定的**
  表達方式與經常出現的字彙

1 注意時間分配

關於 Part 7 的解題，經常聽到考生反映「時間不夠寫不完」。若想提升閱讀測驗的成績，注意時間的分配很重要。閱讀測驗的測驗時間為 75 分鐘，其中 Part 5（單句填空 30 題）和 Part 6（短文填空 16 題）力求每題作答時間為 30 秒，總計 23 分鐘完成，剩下的 52 分鐘用來回答 Part 7 的 54 道題目。只要以一題平均一分鐘以內的速度作答，就能做完 54 道題目。

2 學會解題順序

為了在時間之內做完所有題目，必須學會正確的解題順序。如果讀完文章內容再看題目，無法在一分鐘之內寫完一題。因此，找出職業名稱、時間、地點、價格等「局部搜尋型」的題目，必須「先看題目和選項」，接著只看文章中可導出正確答案的重要段落，這點很重要。

以下介紹最有效率的解題順序。

解題順序

1. 先看題目，弄清楚題目屬於「全文搜尋型」或是「局部搜尋型」。
（詳細說明請見 **3** 了解常見題目形式）

▼

2. 迅速找出與題目有關的段落。
Check! 不需要讀完整個段落，也可以透過標題、粗體字、數字或內含慣用說法的關鍵句導出正確答案。尤其從標題、粗體字、數字等可能 10 秒就可以導出正確答案。對於這類型的題目，以平均一題 40 秒的速度為目標努力吧。

▼

3. 閱讀文章與選項之後作答。
Check! 有些題目比較費時，不清楚答案在哪一個段落，必須整篇看完才能夠作答。正確答案如果是選項 (A) 的話，就不需要再閱讀 (B)、(C)、(D) 的內容。
Check! 選項裡的正確答案大多是文章內容「換句話說」而來，注意這點就能夠找出答案。舉例來說，同樣是「註冊」，有時文章裡使用 registration，選項可能就會改用 enrollment。
Check! 請留意，單篇文章測驗題的最後或倒數第二題經常會出現很難的題目。應考新手別卡在這裡苦思，直接跳過吧。

---

3 了解常見題目形式

出現在 Part 7 的題目有許多類型，這裡將告訴各位如何把代表性的題目分為「局部搜尋型」或「全文搜尋型」。

1. 局部搜尋型或全文搜尋型？
解題的順序是「看完題目之後，從文章中找出題目所問的內容在哪裡，然後對照選項選出正確答案」，不過要從文章中找出導向正確答案的內容，有時必須搜尋全文才找得到。也就是說，題目可分為兩種類型，一種是「全文搜尋型」，一種是從題目的關鍵字即可立刻找出文章中提及該內容之處，也就是「局部搜尋型」。

1. 在全文中搜尋題目提及的地方並導出答案。這種屬於「全文搜尋型」的題目。
① What is indicated [mentioned/stated/suggested] in the form?
（表格中提到了什麼？）

② What can be inferred from the questionnaire?

（從問卷中可以推測出什麼？）

③ What is NOT mentioned in the advertisement?

（廣告中沒有提到什麼？）

④ According to the article, which of the following is true?

（根據文章內容，以下何者為真？）

上述四個例子雖然都是全文搜尋型的題目，但只要記住共通策略，多半也能夠利用局部搜尋的方式導出正確答案。

2. 從題目中找出關鍵字，搜尋關鍵字在文章中出現的位置。這種屬於「局部搜尋型」的題目。

① Who is Mary Smith?

（瑪麗・史密斯是誰？）

[Check!] 職業名稱多半會出現在名字旁邊

② What time does the store open on Tuesdays?

（這家店週二幾點開門營業？）

[Check!] 搜尋寫有時間的部分

③ Where is the head office located?

（總公司位於何處？）

[Check!] 搜尋寫有地點的部分

④ How much does a one-year subscription cost?

（一年的訂閱費用是多少？）

[Check!] 搜尋寫有價格的部分

⑤ Why did Leslie Adams contact Mark Kurzweiler?

（蕾斯莉・亞當斯為什麼聯絡馬克・科茲威勒？）

[Check!] 注意人名，搜尋寫有聯絡原因的部分

☆ 多篇文章測驗分為可從一篇文章找出正確答案的「一篇文章型」，以及必須讀完兩篇或三篇文章才能夠找出正確答案的「兩篇文章型」與「三篇文章型」。詳細內容請見 Day 9。

一個題組有五個問題，其中有三到四題多半只需閱讀單篇文章就能夠找出正確答案。一篇文章型的題目很簡單，也是得分的來源，請務必確實掌握。

2. 常見的代表性題目

1. 問目的：答案大多出現在標題或開頭幾行。
   - What is the purpose of this notice?（這則通知的目的為何？）

2. 題目出現 NOT：多用消去法解題。這種題目比較困難，可先跳過，之後再回頭來寫，才能有效運用時間。
   - What is NOT mentioned in the advertisement?（廣告中沒有提到什麼？）

3. 問同義詞：必須從文章的前後文來判斷，選擇意思最接近的詞彙。
   - In paragraph 1, line 1, the word "affluent" is closest in meaning to
     （第一段第一行的單字 affluent，最接近哪一個意思？）

4. 問具體內容：迅速找出文章中提及題目內容的部分。
   - Who is Ralph Jacobsen?（雷夫·傑可伯森是誰？）

5. 問文章類型：正確答案通常是說明書等手冊。
   - Where would these directions most likely be found?
     （這些使用說明最有可能在哪裡看到？）

6. 問發文者意圖：新制 TOEIC 的閱讀測驗中，增加了從「文字訊息和線上對話」的內容判斷發文者想法的題目。這類題目通常會出現引文，直接引用文章中特定的內容，可從前後文讀出發文者的想法。
   - At XX A.M., what does XXXX most likely mean when she writes, "..."?
     （上午 XX 時，XXXX 寫「⋯⋯」最有可能是什麼意思？）

7. 問插入句的位置：這也是新題型。可從插入句的連接詞、副詞、定冠詞、指示代名詞、慣用說法導出正確答案。
   - In which of the positions marked [1], [2], [3], and [4] does the following sentence best belong?（下列句子最適合放在 [1], [2], [3], [4] 哪一個位置？）

以下舉出能夠從插入句的關鍵字、關鍵句等導出正確答案的範例。
① 連接詞與副詞
   - 插入句若出現 however, although, but, yet, on the other hand 等表示轉折的連接詞，表示前文是與插入句意思相反的內容。
   - 插入句若出現副詞 similarly，表示前文是與插入句意思相似的內容。
   - 插入句若出現副詞 therefore，表示前文是原因。
   - 插入句若出現副詞 also, additionally, furthermore，表示前文也有同樣的內容。

② 定冠詞

- 插入句若出現定冠詞 the 加上名詞，表示前文有不定冠詞 a/an 加上該名詞，或是有該名詞的複數形。

  例 the investor（該投資者）→表示前文有 an investor 或 investors

③ 指示代名詞（包括指示詞、指示代名詞、所有格等）

- 插入句若出現指示代名詞，表示前文有該代名詞所指涉的內容。

  例 it →表示前文有 it 所指涉的內容

  this tendency（這個傾向）→表示前文有說明該傾向為何的內容

  these five kinds（這五個種類）→表示前文出現了五個種類

  her method（她的方法）→表示前文有女子的名字與方法

  several other shoppers（其他好幾個購物的人）

  →表示前文提到與購物的人有關的內容

④ 慣用說法

- 插入句若出現 Please be advised of a change to the bus service.（公車服務內容有異動，請注意。）等表示通知的慣用說法，表示後面有具體的例子。
- 插入句若出現 Please contact me personally if you have any questions.（如有任何疑問，請私下與我聯絡。）後面很可能會出現個人的聯絡方式。

4 分辨文章類型，快速找出正確答案

Part 7 涵蓋各類型的文章，只要了解常見的文章類型，就能夠快速找出題目問的內容在哪裡。本書將以「天」為單位，每天學習一種文章類型的閱讀重點。

共通策略

1. 注意標題、粗體字與數字，通常就能夠導出正確答案。
2. 從文章的開頭與最後、開頭的兩到三行，以及各個段落第一句與最後一句，通常能夠導出正確答案。

   重要 「掌握重點」和「推測」的題目，正確答案出現在文章的開頭與結尾，這是因為「最想說的內容」多寫在開頭與結尾。只要能連接開頭與結尾的內容，多半都能夠掌握重點。
3. 聯絡方式（電子郵件、電話、郵寄等）、截止日期、可能獲得資訊的地點等，大多出現在文章最後。

---

4. 要注意各類型文章的版面格式。
5. 對照文章內的項目閱讀。
6. Note、P.S. 裡經常會出現正確答案。

5 依據文章類型，找出該類型固定的表達方式與經常出現的字彙

有時只要先熟悉電子郵件、信件、通知等會使用哪些固定的表達方式，記住關鍵句，幾秒鐘就能夠導出正確答案。配合每一天介紹的文章類型，記住這些關鍵句吧。

透過本書能夠知道常見題目形式，了解文章類型，並學會各類型文章的慣用說法和常用單字，這就是 Part 7 最佳的應考對策。只要懂得這些策略，各位就能夠大幅提高閱讀測驗的分數。

最後整理時間方面的建議。

TOEIC L&R TEST 是一場與時間的戰鬥，「時間不夠寫不完」是許多考生共同的煩惱。Part 7 的單篇文章測驗中，一開始的幾道題目比較簡單，接著是中等難度，最後兩、三題比較困難，最難的題目會有一題。至於雙篇和三篇文章測驗，也有 80% 的題目屬於比較簡單的題目。不管題目的難易程度為何，得分都是一樣的。短文較多簡單的題目。難題可先跳過，最後再解題。有技巧地分配時間，就能夠戰勝這場與時間的戰鬥！

✳ CONTENTS

Day 1

本日主題
● 廣告

廣告題經常出現服飾、家具、家電用品等商品的宣傳，以及餐廳、飯店、旅行社、房屋仲介、美術館等的服務或講座宣傳（徵才廣告將在 Day 6 介紹）。

遇到廣告題，請先確認這是「誰（廣告主）」基於「什麼目的」所做的廣告。

STEP 1 看看這類文章的閱讀重點！

● 家具行結束營業大拍賣的廣告

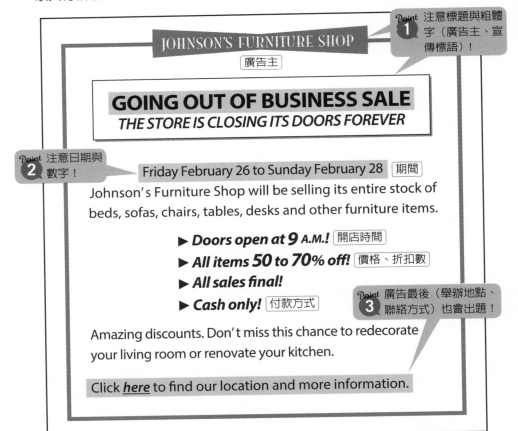

Point 1 注意標題與粗體字（廣告主、宣傳標語）！

JOHNSON'S FURNITURE SHOP 廣告主

GOING OUT OF BUSINESS SALE
THE STORE IS CLOSING ITS DOORS FOREVER

Point 2 注意日期與數字！

Friday February 26 to Sunday February 28 期間
Johnson's Furniture Shop will be selling its entire stock of beds, sofas, chairs, tables, desks and other furniture items.

▶ **Doors open at 9** A.M.! 開店時間
▶ **All items 50 to 70% off!** 價格、折扣數
▶ **All sales final!**
▶ **Cash only!** 付款方式

Point 3 廣告最後（舉辦地點、聯絡方式）也會出題！

Amazing discounts. Don't miss this chance to redecorate your living room or renovate your kitchen.

Click *here* to find our location and more information.

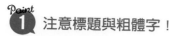

Point 1 注意標題與粗體字！

廣告最上面的標題與粗體字寫有廣告主（公司名、店名等）或宣傳標語。首先從這裡大致掌握「廣告主」、「廣告目的」、「舉辦活動的原因」和「廣告對象」。

Point 2 注意日期與數字！

題目經常問到商店的營業日、營業時間 (hours of operation, business hours)、展覽或特賣會的活動期間與時間、商品價格、折扣數等，可分別從廣告上的日期與數字導出答案。

Point 3 最後的資訊也要注意！

聯絡方式、申請方式（電話號碼、電子信箱、網址等）、特賣會的舉辦地點 (location)、商品付款方式等補充資訊，大多寫在廣告最後。相關資訊的洽詢單位則會寫在 To obtain more information（想獲得更多資訊）、For more info（更多資訊）等字詞後面。

中譯

強森家具行

結束營業大拍賣
本店將結束營業

2 月 26 日（五）至 2 月 28 日（日）
強森家具行將出清床具、沙發、桌椅及其他家具商品。

▶ 早上九點開始營業！
▶ 所有商品三折到五折優惠！
▶ 最後出清折扣！
▶ 限現金交易！

不可思議的折扣。別錯過這次機會，趕快重新裝飾你的客廳，或改建你的廚房。

點選此處了解我們的位置及更多資訊。

1　與舉辦特賣會的原因及廣告主有關的題目
通常一開始就會問舉辦特賣會或打折的原因，或是與廣告主有關的問題。請記住標題與文中特有的表達方式。

題目

- Why is the bargain sale being held?（為什麼要舉辦特賣會？）
- Why have the prices been reduced?（為什麼要調低價格？）

文中的表達方式

- Grand opening from May 10th to 15th!（5 月 10 日至 15 日盛大開幕！）
- ABC Store is closing its doors forever. / ABC Store is going out of business.（ABC 商店即將結束營業。）
- Super Energy Drink has just been launched!（超能飲料新上市！）
- The 5th Anniversary Sale!（五週年慶特賣！）
- Welcome to the beautifully renovated Sunrise Hotel!（歡迎來到整修後美輪美奐的日出飯店！）
- Winter clearance sale has just begun!（冬季出清特賣剛剛開始！）
- Overstocked Items at Huge Savings.（省很大商場出清庫存。）

2　與廣告對象有關的題目
廣告對象出乎意料也經常出題。

題目

- Who is this advertisement intended for?（這則廣告的對象是誰？）

文中的表達方式

- Members only!（僅限會員！）
- Ace Consulting Co. offers workshops to (new employees / company executives / small business owners).
（王牌顧問公司為〔新進員工 / 公司主管 / 小型企業主〕舉辦工作坊。）

3　與付款方式有關的題目
cash（現金）、checks（支票）、credit card（信用卡）等常見的付款方式請務必牢記。

題目

- What forms of payments are accepted?（他們接受哪些付款方式？）

文中的表達方式

- Cash, checks and major credit card payments are accepted.
  （接受現金、支票和各大信用卡付款。）
- We accept cash, major credit cards or bank transfers, but unfortunately we can't accept checks.
  （我們接受現金、各大信用卡或銀行轉帳付款，但很抱歉無法接受支票。）

4 與取得資訊的方法或申請方式有關的題目
不管哪一種廣告都一樣，聯絡方式、申請方式大多寫在最後。

題目

- According to the advertisement, how can more information be obtained?
  （根據廣告內容，如何獲得更多資訊？）

文中的表達方式

- For more information, visit us online at www.oldworldcruises.com.
  （想了解更多資訊，請上我們的網站 www.oldworldcruises.com。）
- To make reservations, e-mail us at oldworldinfo@world.eu.
  （如欲訂位，請傳送電子郵件至 oldworldinfo@world.eu。）

加分表現

有時候打折是因為商品本身有問題，例如瑕疵品，或者原本是樣品、展示品等。如果是這種情況，文中的表達方式在選項裡如何換句話說呢？

1. 商品是瑕疵品時
   正文 minor scratches（有輕微刮痕）
   → 選項 defective items（瑕疵商品）

2. 商品是樣品、展示品時
   正文 Get 50% off on showroom items.（展示商品打對折。）
   → 選項 floor model（店內樣品、展示品）

3. 商品已經停產時
   正文 Italian chairs #12st5467 have been discontinued.
   （義大利製的椅子 #12st5467 已經停產了。）
   → 選項 be no longer produced（已經不再生產了）

Questions 1-3 refer to the following advertisement.

ANDOVER Hotel
at the Convention Center

ANDOVER Hotel provides all of the amenities and services expected of a premier hotel, with four types of rooms to meet your price range and lodging needs: Standard, Superior, and Deluxe Doubles, as well as our Executive Suites that feature a refrigerator and well-stocked bar.

- All rooms equipped with desks and telephones with voice-mail

- WiFi accessible throughout all facilities

- Fitness center open 24 hours a day

- Early check-in and late check-out available to all convention-goers

**Log on to our Web site or call
ANDOVER (263-6837) to make a reservation today.**

1. Who is likely to stay at the Andover Hotel?

    (A) Families
    (B) Holiday travelers
    (C) Conference attendees
    (D) Company executives

2. What is true of the Andover Hotel?

    (A) It is located downtown.
    (B) It offers free laundry service.
    (C) It has a swimming pool and sauna.
    (D) It provides Internet access.

3. What is stated about the fitness center?

    (A) An experienced trainer is present.
    (B) It is available to guests all day long.
    (C) Users must show their guest cards.
    (D) A reservation is required.

中譯 問題 1-3：請看以下廣告。

[1]安多佛飯店
會議中心館

安多佛飯店提供各種高級飯店必備的設施及服務，四種房型能配合您的預算及住宿需求：標準客房、精緻客房、豪華雙人房與商務套房，其中商務套房還配備了冰箱及備貨齊全的酒吧。

- 所有房型皆備有書桌，以及具語音留言功能的電話。
- [2]全館皆有無線網路。
- [3]健身中心 24 小時開放。
- 所有[1]參加會議者皆可提早入住或延後退房。

請登入我們的網站，或撥打安多佛專線 (263-6837)，今天就預約訂房。

單字

- □ convention center 會議中心
- □ amenity 名 便利的設施（常用複數形）
- □ premier 形 首要的，第一的
- □ price range 價格帶
- □ lodge 動 住宿
- □ standard 形 標準的
- □ superior 形 上等的，優良的
- □ deluxe 形 豪華的
- □ executive 形 商務的，高級的
- □ suite 名 套房
- □ feature 動 以…為特色
- □ accessible 形 可取得的，可利用的
- □ facility 名 設施，設備
- □ make a reservation 預約，預定

解答 1. (C) 2. (D) 3. (B)

1. 誰有可能入住安多佛飯店？
(A) 家庭客
(B) 渡假旅客
(C) 參加會議者
(D) 公司主管

解說 注意標題與粗體字 （難易度）★ ★

從標題 ANDOVER Hotel at the Convention Center（安多佛飯店會議中心館）可知，飯店位於會議中心內。另外，從方框內第四點的 convention-goers（參加會議者）可進一步推測，參加會議的人可能入住該飯店，因此正確答案是 (C) Conference attendees。

2. 關於安多佛飯店的敘述，何者為真？
(A) 位於市中心。
(B) 提供免費的洗衣服務。
(C) 有游泳池和三溫暖。
(D) 提供網路服務。

解說 注意條列項目 （難易度）★

從方框內第二點的 WiFi accessible throughout all facilities（全館皆有無線網路）可知，飯店提供網路服務，因此正確答案是 (D) It provides Internet access.。

換句話說 正文 WiFi accessible ➡ 選項 provides Internet access

3. 文中關於健身中心有何敘述？
(A) 現場有經驗豐富的教練。
(B) 整天都開放給房客使用。
(C) 使用者必須出示貴賓卡。
(D) 需要預約。

解說 找出 fitness center （難易度）★

從方框內第三點的 Fitness center open 24 hours a day（健身中心 24 小時開放）可知，健身中心整天都可以使用，因此正確答案是 (B) It is available to guests all day long.。

換句話說 正文 open 24 hours a day ➡ 選項 is available to guests all day long

Questions 1-3 refer to the following advertisement.

Ron's
Garage

DISCOUNT COUPON

GOOD FOR 1 OIL CHANGE FOR $20
(25% OFF NORMAL PRICE)
APRIL 1 TO APRIL 30

Now that winter is behind us,
let Ron's expert mechanics
get your motor ready for summer
with a quick 10-minute oil change.
Includes no-cost installation of a new oil filter.
Bring this coupon to the downtown location only.
No reservation needed.

Hours of Operation:	
Monday - Wednesday	7 A.M. - 7 P.M.
Friday	6 A.M. - 7 P.M.
Saturday - Sunday	8 A.M. - 7 P.M.
Thursday	Closed

Ron's Garage at 4 Locations:
- Junction of Highway 46 and Baker Street
- Intersection of Main and Broadway downtown
- Exit 34 of Interstate I-99
- Airport Way

1. What is NOT mentioned in the advertisement?

(A) A discount in price
(B) Fast service
(C) A tire change
(D) A free installation

2. Where is this discount auto service being offered?

(A) Junction of Highway 46 and Baker Street
(B) Intersection of Main and Broadway downtown
(C) Exit 34 of Interstate I-99
(D) Airport Way

3. When does the garage open on Tuesdays?

(A) At 6 A.M.
(B) At 7 A.M.
(C) At 8 A.M.
(D) At 9 A.M.

中譯 問題 1-3：請看以下廣告。

榮恩修車廠
[1]折價券
換油一次 20 美元
（原價打 75 折）
4 月 1 日至 4 月 30 日

冬天已過，讓榮恩的專業技師為您的愛車做好迎接夏天的準備，
[1]快速換油只要 10 分鐘。包含免費安裝新的機油濾清器。
[2]僅限攜帶此折價券至市中心分店。
不需預約。

營業時間：
[3]週一至週三　早上 7 點到晚上 7 點
週五　　　　　早上 6 點到晚上 7 點
週六、週日　　早上 8 點到晚上 7 點
週四　　　　　公休

榮恩修車廠四家分店：
- 46 號高速公路與貝克街口
- [2]市中心緬因路與百老匯道交叉口
- I-99 號州際公路 34 號出口
- 機場路

單字

- □ garage 名 修車廠
- □ discount coupon 折價券
- □ normal price 原價
- □ mechanic 名 技師
- □ no-cost 形 免費的
- □ installation 名 安裝
- □ oil filter 機油濾清器
- □ location 名 位置，店點
- □ junction 名（兩道路的）會合處
- □ intersection 名（道路的）交叉口
- □ interstate 名 州際公路

解答 1. (C)   2. (B)   3. (B)

1. 廣告中沒有提到什麼？
(A) 價格折扣
(B) 快速服務
(C) 更換輪胎
(D) 免費安裝

解說 NOT 問句通常可用消去法解題

（難易度）★

從標題的 DISCOUNT COUPON（折價券）可知，廣告與價格折扣有關；正文第一句的 a quick 10-minute oil change（快速換油只要 10 分鐘）提及快速服務，第二句 no-cost installation（免費安裝）提及免費安裝，分別與選項 (A)、(B)、(D) 相符。廣告沒有提到的是 (C) A tire change，為正確答案。

2. 哪一家修車廠提供汽車保養服務的折扣？
(A) 46 號高速公路與貝克街口
(B) 市中心緬因路與百老匯道交叉口
(C) I-99 號州際公路 34 號出口
(D) 機場路

解說 找出 location 並注意有 only 的句子

（難易度）★★

從廣告正文第三句的 Bring this coupon to the downtown location only.（僅限攜帶此折價券至市中心分店。）可知，折價券只能在市中心分店使用，而從 4 Locations（四家分店）可知共四家分店，其中 Intersection of Main and Broadway downtown（市中心緬因路與百老匯道交叉口）位於市中心，因此正確答案是 (B)。

3. 修車廠週二幾點開始營業？
(A) 早上 6 點
(B) 早上 7 點
(C) 早上 8 點
(D) 早上 9 點

解說 找出 Hours of Operation   （難易度）★

Hours of Operation（營業時間）標示著 Monday-Wednesday 7 A.M. - 7 P.M.（週一至週三早上 7 點到晚上 7 點），可知週二是早上 7 點開店，因此正確答案是 (B) At 7 A.M.。

Questions 1-4 refer to the following advertisement.

Old World Cruises

Exploring the Old World in Comfort and Ease

If you like ocean cruises on the Caribbean or Mediterranean seas or on the Pacific Ocean, you will love river cruises because the best way to visit some of Europe's most fascinating and beautiful sights is by boat. Travel aboard luxurious ships in spacious staterooms with large windows. Watch the landscape glide by on the Rhine, the Elbe, the Ebro, the Seine, and other famous old world rivers.

Almost everything is included in the package price: deluxe accommodations on the boat, all onboard meals, daily shore excursions, cultural enrichment activities such as museum visits, and free ship-wide WiFi access.

An all-inclusive river cruise costs less per day than you might otherwise spend for hotels alone. With Old World Cruises, you pay in U.S. dollars, and once you have paid, you have no further worries about currency fluctuations, fuel surcharges, taxes or anything else. Packages also include:

- **A discount of $200 per person for tours of 5 days or more**
- **Onboard health, exercise, and medical facilities**
- **Complimentary beverage with dinner**

To make reservations or obtain more information, see your travel agent, e-mail us at oldworldinfo@world.eu, or visit www.oldworldcruises.com.

1. Where are the cruises mentioned in this advertisement?

    (A) On lakes

    (B) On rivers

    (C) On oceans

    (D) On coasts

2. What is most likely NOT included in the package price?

    (A) Trips to the shore

    (B) Dinners on the boat

    (C) Airfare to departure point

    (D) Nightly room charge

3. How can passengers receive a reduced price?

    (A) By booking longer cruises

    (B) By touring in groups of five or more

    (C) By traveling during the off-season

    (D) By taking more than one cruise

4. What is NOT stated in the advertisement as a way to request more information?

    (A) Sending an e-mail

    (B) Making a telephone call

    (C) Accessing a Web site

    (D) Contacting a travel agent

練習題 3 答案與解說

中譯 問題 1-4：請看以下廣告。

舊大陸遊輪
輕鬆舒適探索舊大陸

如果您喜歡搭乘加勒比海、地中海或太平洋的海上遊輪，[1]您也會喜愛河上遊輪，因為參觀歐洲某些最迷人、最美麗景點的方式，便是乘船遊覽。搭乘豪華遊輪，坐在配有大片窗戶的特等艙寬敞空間裡，悠遊萊茵河、易北河、埃布羅河、塞納河與其他著名的舊大陸的河流，欣賞流動而過的岸邊風景。

套裝價格幾乎包含了所有消費：[2]船上豪華的艙房、所有船上餐點、每日岸上遊覽、參觀博物館等提高文化涵養的活動，以及免費的全船無線網路。

全包式河上遊輪每日的費用比單純住飯店的費用還要低廉。參加舊大陸遊輪行程，您必須以美金支付，付款後，便不用再擔憂匯率變動、燃油附加費、稅金或其他費用。套裝行程也包含：

- [3]每人 200 美元折價券，可用於五日（含）以上的行程
- 使用船上的健康、運動及醫療設施
- 免費的晚餐飲料

[4]如欲訂位或獲得更多資訊，請洽旅行社，或是傳送電子郵件至 oldworldinfo@world.eu，或上網 www.oldworldcruises.com。

單字

- □ cruise 名 乘船旅行
- □ explore 動 探索
- □ ease 名 舒適，自在
- □ fascinating 形 迷人的
- □ luxurious 形 豪華的
- □ spacious 形 寬敞的
- □ stateroom 名（遊輪的）特等艙
- □ landscape 名 景色
- □ glide by 流動而過
- □ accommodation 名 住宿設施
  （美式英文多用複數形）

- □ shore excursion 上岸觀光
- □ cultural enrichment activity
  提高文化涵養的活動
- □ all-inclusive 形 全部包含在內的
- □ otherwise 副 用其他方法
- □ currency 名 貨幣
- □ fluctuation 名 波動，變動
- □ fuel surcharge 燃油附加費
- □ complimentary 形 贈送的
- □ beverage 名 飲料
- □ agent 名 代理人

解答 1. (B)　2. (C)　3. (A)　4. (B)

1. 廣告中提到的遊輪在哪裡航行？
(A) 在湖上
(B) 在河上
(C) 在海上
(D) 在沿岸

解說 注意文章的開頭　（難易度）★

從第一段第一句的 If you like ocean cruises on the Caribbean or Mediterranean seas or on the Pacific Ocean, you will love river cruises...（如果您喜歡搭乘加勒比海、地中海或太平洋的海上遊輪，您也會喜愛河上遊輪……）可知，這是乘船遊河的廣告，因此正確答案是 (B) On rivers。

2. 套裝價格中，最有可能不包含哪一項？
(A) 岸上旅遊
(B) 船上晚餐
(C) 到出發點的機票
(D) 過夜的房價

解說 找出 package price；NOT 問句通常可用消去法解題　（難易度）★★

從第二段 package price（套裝價格）後面的內容可知，套裝價格包含 deluxe accommodations（豪華的艙房）、onboard meals（船上餐點）和 shore excursions（岸上遊覽），分別與選項 (D)、(B)、(A) 相符，不包含在內的是機票，因此正確答案是 (C) Airfare to departure point。

3. 乘客如何取得折扣價格？
(A) 預訂較長的航程
(B) 五人（含）以上組團參加
(C) 淡季的時候旅遊
(D) 參加一個以上的航程

解說 注意折扣金額的數字　（難易度）★★

折扣條件大多與折扣數寫在一起。從條列項目第一點的 for tours of 5 days or more（用於五日〔含〕以上的行程）可知，未滿五天無法享有折扣，也就是說，預約較長的航程可享折扣，因此正確答案是 (A) By booking longer cruises。

換句話說　正文 tours of 5 days or more ➡ 選項 longer cruises

4. 廣告提到取得更多資訊的方式，其中不包含哪一項？
(A) 傳送電子郵件
(B) 打電話
(C) 連上網站
(D) 聯絡旅行社

解說 注意最後寫有相關資訊洽詢單位（聯絡方式）的部分　（難易度）★

從廣告最後 obtain more information（獲得更多資訊）後面的內容可知，see your travel agent（請洽旅行社）、e-mail us（傳送電子郵件）、visit（瀏覽網站）皆為取得資訊的方法，分別與選項 (D)、(A)、(C) 相符，廣告中沒有提到打電話，因此正確答案是 (B) Making a telephone call。

1 分鐘 CHECK!

複習「廣告」的閱讀重點及 Day 1 的必背字彙。

「廣告」的閱讀重點

- ☐ 廣告題經常出現服飾、家具、家電用品等商品的宣傳，以及餐廳、飯店、旅行社、房屋仲介、美術館等的服務或講座宣傳。

- ☐ 首先從廣告最上面的標題與粗體字大致掌握「廣告主」、「廣告目的」、「舉辦活動的原因」、「廣告對象」。

- ☐ 注意商店的營業日、營業時間、商品價格、折扣數等與日期、數字有關的資訊。

- ☐ 聯絡方式、申請方式（電話號碼、電子信箱、網址等）、特賣會的舉辦地點、商品付款方式等資訊通常寫在廣告最後。

「廣告」的必背字彙

- ☐ stock 名 庫存
- ☐ Doors open at... ……點開門營業。
- ☐ discount coupon 折價券
- ☐ location 名 位置，店點
- ☐ hours of operation 營業時間
- ☐ Log on to our Web site. 連上我們的網站。
- ☐ normal price 原價
- ☐ include 動 包含
- ☐ no-cost 形 免費的
- ☐ complimentary 形 贈送的

Day 2

本日主題

● 表單（繳費通知單、申請表）

表單包含繳費通知單、申請表、訂單、問卷、時程表、圖表、菜單等，其中常出現在測驗中的是公共費用的繳費通知單，以及報章雜誌的訂閱申請表。

閱讀繳費通知單時，請找出「目的」、「日期」、「費用」、「繳費期限」與「聯絡方式」。

STEP 1 看看這類文章的閱讀重點！

● 有線電視收視費繳費通知單

Point 1 注意標題！

Metropolitan Cable Television

P.O. Box 7180
Auckland

Point 2 記住必定出現的項目！

帳號　　　　　　　October 1 日期
Account Number 143731　　Service: 30 channel premier plan

Summary 概要	Outstanding Balance from 9/25 未付清的餘款	Current Charges 目前費用	Total Due 應付總額
Charges 費用	$0	$42	$42
Due Date 繳費期限	October 25		
Payment Type 繳費方式	Automatic Withdrawal from bank	Full amount	
Service Address 收視地點	194 7th St. Auckland		

STATEMENT REFLECTS TRANSACTIONS MADE FROM 9/1 TO 9/30

Note: If you have any questions about your bill, please call Customer Service: 1-888-555-6498.

Point 3 注意表格外的資訊（聯絡方式）！

看標題掌握概要！

表單上方的標題有公司名稱，通常可從這裡看出表單的種類（公共費用繳費通知單、雜誌定期訂閱申請表等）。不用全篇讀完，先看標題，如果沒有標題就從與題目有關的項目或關鍵字等來掌握概要。

 記住每一種表單必定會出現的項目，找出該項目！

繳費通知單和訂單上面固定會有費用 (charge)、日期 (date)、繳費方式 (payment type)、繳費期限 (due date / deadline) 等項目。以下繳費通知單之外的表單也要確認。

- 問卷、申請表（列出的項目、列出的內容）
- 時程表（日期、活動內容、執行者等）
- 菜單（菜色、價格）

 注意表格外的資訊！

表單中表格以外的 Note、P.S.、Comments、粗體字、斜體字等，寫有聯絡方式、逾期繳費時採取的措施等資訊。

中譯

大都會有線電視
奧克蘭 7180 號信箱
10 月 1 日

帳號 143731　　　購買服務：30 頻道基本方案

概要	9 月 25 日起未付清的餘款	目前費用	應付總額
費用	$0	$42	$42
繳費期限	10 月 25 日		
繳費方式	銀行帳戶自動扣款	全額	
收視地點	奧克蘭第七街 194 號		
上述為 9 月 1 日至 9 月 30 日之交易			
注意：若您對帳單內容有任何疑問，請撥打客服專線：1-888-555-6498。			

1 與時程表、圖表、申請表的目的有關的題目

表單題可分為「問主旨」以及「問詳情」兩種題型。問主旨的話，通常只要看標題或開頭就能夠知道。在正確答案的選項裡，通常與 show 一起使用，如：to show the flight schedule（列出班機時間）。

題目

- What is the main purpose of this (schedule/chart / application form)?
  （這份〔時程表／圖表／申請表〕的主要目的為何？）

文中的表達方式

- 標題 Domestic Flight Time Table to and from Chicago
  （來往芝加哥的國內班機時刻表）

  ⬇

  答案 to show the flight schedule（列出班機時間）

- 標題 Tour of Production Facility（生產設施的參觀導覽）

  ⬇

  答案 to show the procedure for visiting a factory（列出參觀工廠的流程）

- 標題 Sales figures by regions in the last year（去年一整年各地區的銷售數字）

  ⬇

  答案 to show the past year's sales figures（列出去年的銷售數字）

- 標題 Subscription Renewal Notice（續訂通知）

  ⬇

  答案 to encourage a current customer to renew a subscription
  （鼓勵現有客戶續訂）

2 與繳費期限和日期有關的題目

關於繳費期限，date（日期）、deadline 和 due date（繳費期限）很重要。這類詳細資訊必須先看題目，再配合表格裡的項目找出正確答案。

題目

- By what date should this bill be paid?（這份帳單應該在什麼時候以前繳？）
- When is the deadline?（繳費期限是什麼時候？）

文中的表達方式

- Due Date: November 30（繳費期限：11 月 30 日）
- P.S. Your payment is due at the end of the first month of your new subscription.（附註：繳費期限為續訂開始後第一個月的最後一天。）

3 與取得資訊的方式、申請方式、注意事項有關的題目
聯絡方式、申請方式、逾期繳費時的注意事項等，通常寫在文章最後。

題目

- How can more information be obtained?（如何獲得更多資訊？）

文中的表達方式

- Note: If you have any questions about your bill, please call Customer Service: 1-888-555-6498.
  （若您對帳單內容有任何疑問，請撥打客服專線：1-888-555-6498。）
- Mail or fax this application form to *San Francisco Monthly*.
  （請將本申請表以郵寄或傳真方式送至《舊金山月刊》。）

加分表現

★ 訂閱申請表、繳費通知單、訂單的關鍵字

題目問到「詳細資訊」時，必須從文章裡快速找出對應的項目，導出正確答案，因此務必記住文章中可能出現的關鍵字。

1. 關於訂閱申請表
   - subscription 名 訂閱
   - renew 動 更新
   - issue 名（雜誌、期刊等的）期，號
   - cover/newsstand/regular price 定價
   - subscriber 名 訂閱者
   - renewal 名 更新

2. 關於繳費通知單、訂單
   - billing date 請款日
   - item 名 商品名稱
   - total 名 總計
   - installment payment 分期付款
   - quantity 名 數量
   - balance 名 餘款
   - pay in full 一次付清
   - partial payment 部分付款

Questions 1-3 refer to the following bill.

PACIFIC POWER

Billing Date: January 5
Account Number: 050626
Due Date: January 31

Service Period	Amount used this month (kilowatts per hour)	Amount used last month	Cost current month
12/1 - 12/31	1,640 kwh	1,520 kwh	$112

$112	Current month charges
$103	Past due (previous month)
$ 0	Interest on balance
$215	Net amount due

Note: A 6% interest charge is assessed on all outstanding balances more than one month past due.

1. By what date should this bill be paid?

    (A) December 1
    (B) December 31
    (C) January 5
    (D) January 31

2. How much should the customer pay for energy use during the month of December?

    (A) $0
    (B) $103
    (C) $112
    (D) $215

3. According to the bill, what happens when a payment is more than a month late?

    (A) An interest charge is added.
    (B) A flat fee must be paid.
    (C) Service is suspended.
    (D) Legal action is taken.

中譯 問題 1-3：請看以下帳單。

太平洋電力

請款日：1 月 5 日

帳號：050626

[1]繳費期限：1 月 31 日

使用期間	本月使用量 （每小時千瓦）	前月使用量	本月費用
12/1-12/31	1,640 千瓦	1,520 千瓦	[2]$112

$112 本月費用

$103 逾期未付費用（前月）

$0 未付清的餘款之利息

$215 應付淨額

注意：[3]超過一個月未付清的餘款將收取 6% 的利息。

單字

- □ account number 帳號
- □ period 名 期間
- □ amount 名 量
- □ current month 本月
- □ past due 逾期未付費用

- □ interest 名 利息
- □ net 形 淨值的
- □ assess 動 課以（一定費用）
- □ outstanding balance 未付清的餘款

解答 **1.** (D) **2.** (C) **3.** (A)

---

1. 這份帳單應該在什麼時候以前繳？
- (A) 12 月 1 日
- (B) 12 月 31 日
- (C) 1 月 5 日
- (D) 1 月 31 日

解說 找出 Due Date　　　　（難易度）★

從表單右上方的 Due Date（繳費期限）可知，應在 1 月 31 日前繳費，因此正確答案是 (D) January 31。請記住「繳費期限」、「請款日」等繳費通知單常用的詞彙。

---

2. 這位客戶 12 月應支付多少電費？
- (A) $0
- (B) $103
- (C) $112
- (D) $215

解說 找出 Cost current month　（難易度）★

表格中的 Service Period（使用期間）寫著 12/1-12/31，表示 Cost current month（本月費用）顯示的是 12 月的費用，也就是 112 美元，因此正確答案是 (C) $112。從表格下方的 Current month charges（本月費用）也可知道答案。

---

3. 根據帳單內容，費用逾期未繳超過一個月會發生什麼事？
- (A) 另外收取利息。
- (B) 必須支付固定費用。
- (C) 暫停供電。
- (D) 採取法律行動。

解說 注意 Note　　　　　（難易度）★★

Note 部分寫 A 6% interest charge is assessed on all outstanding balances more than one month past due.（超過一個月未付清的餘款將收取 6% 的利息。）也就是說逾期超過一個月將會被收取利息，因此正確答案是 (A) An interest charge is added.。

換句話說　[正文] is assessed ➡ [選項] is added

Questions 1-3 refer to the following form.

POSTAGE
PAID
PERMIT NO.1

WORLD NEWS WEEKLY
Subscription Renewal Notice

Dear Reader,

Your subscription to *World News Weekly* will expire at the end of this month. Save 50% off the newsstand price by re-subscribing now. Fill in the information below and simply drop this card in a mailbox (postage is pre-paid).

Don't let events pass you by!

_____ Name _____ Subscriber Number

☐ **Two years (100 issues) €400** ☐ **One year (50 issues) €220**

☐ **Six months (25 issues) €130** ☐ **Three months (12 issues) €80**

Preferred Billing:

☐ **Personal check**   ☐ **Postal money order**   ☐ **Bank transfer (electronic check)**

P.S. Your payment is due at the end of the first month of your new subscription.

1. What is the purpose of this form?

(A) To attract new subscribers

(B) To collect an overdue payment

(C) To encourage a subscription renewal

(D) To announce an advertising campaign

2. How much does a one-year subscription cost?

(A) €400

(B) €220

(C) €130

(D) €80

3. What is NOT indicated in this form?

(A) The form must be sent by mail.

(B) The magazine is published weekly.

(C) The subscriber can get a discount.

(D) Payment by credit card is preferred.

中譯 問題 1-3：請看以下表單。

郵資已付
1 號許可證

[3]世界新聞週刊
[1]續訂通知

親愛的讀者：

您訂閱的《世界新聞週刊》將於本月底到期，[3]現在續訂可享有定價的半價折扣。只要填寫以下表格，並[3]將此卡片投入郵筒即可（郵資已付）。

別錯過世界大事！

姓名 ＿＿＿＿＿＿＿＿＿＿　訂閱編號 ＿＿＿＿＿＿＿＿＿

□ 兩年（100 期）　400 歐元　　　　□ [2]一年（50 期）　220 歐元
□ 六個月（25 期）　130 歐元　　　　□ 三個月（12 期）　80 歐元

偏好付款方式：
□ 個人支票　　　　　　□ 郵政匯票　　　　　　□ 銀行轉帳（電子支票）

附註：繳費期限為續訂開始後第一個月的最後一天。

單字

□ postage 名 郵資	□ drop 動 投遞
□ permit 名 許可證	□ check 名 支票
□ expire 動 到期	□ preferred 形 偏好的，優先的
□ re-subscribe 動 續訂	□ postal money order 郵政匯票
□ fill in... 填寫…	□ bank transfer 銀行轉帳

解答 **1.** (C)　**2.** (B)　**3.** (D)

1. 這份表單的目的為何？
(A) 吸引新訂戶
(B) 收取逾期費用
(C) 鼓勵續訂
(D) 宣布宣傳活動

解說　注意標題　　　　　　　難易度 ★

從標題 Subscription Renewal Notice（續訂通知）可知，這是通知續訂的表單。從正文第二句 Save 50% off the newsstand price by re-subscribing now.（現在續訂可享有定價的半價折扣。）可知，該週刊用促銷活動鼓勵現有訂戶續訂，因此正確答案是 (C) To encourage a subscription renewal。

換句話說　正文 re-subscribing ➡ 選項 subscription renewal

2. 訂閱一年要多少錢？
(A) 400 歐元
(B) 220 歐元
(C) 130 歐元
(D) 80 歐元

解說　對照表單裡的 One year 與訂閱費用，找出答案　　難易度 ★

表單中共列出四個訂閱期間供選擇，One year（一年）要 220 歐元，也就是說，訂閱一年的費用是 220 歐元，因此正確答案是 (B) €220。

3. 表單中沒有指出什麼？
(A) 這份表單必須以郵寄方式送出。
(B) 雜誌每週出刊。
(C) 訂閱者可以享有折扣。
(D) 希望訂閱者以信用卡付款。

解說　注意粗體字；NOT 問句通常可用消去法解題　　難易度 ★★

從標題的 WORLD NEWS WEEKLY（《世界新聞週刊》）可知雜誌每週出刊；正文第二、三句分別提到 50% off（半價折扣）和 drop this card in a mailbox（將此卡片投入郵筒），分別與選項 (B)、(C)、(A) 相符。表單中列出三種付款方式，其中並不包含信用卡付款，因此正確答案是 (D) Payment by credit card is preferred.。

Questions 1-3 refer to the following questionnaire.

Community Clinic
(Serving our city since 1975)

— PATIENT QUESTIONNAIRE —

1. How long did you wait to see a physician or health care specialist today?
   - ☐ less than 30 minutes
   - ☐ from 30 minutes to 1 hour
   - ☐ from 1 hour to 90 minutes
   - ☑ more than 90 minutes

2. How would you rate the quality of treatment from your physician or health care specialist today?
   - ☑ excellent
   - ☐ good
   - ☐ fair
   - ☐ unsatisfactory
   - ☐ poor

3. How would you rate the quality of service from the receptionists and the accounting department?
   - ☐ excellent
   - ☐ good
   - ☐ fair
   - ☑ unsatisfactory
   - ☐ poor

4. After your treatment, how long did it take for your bill to be ready?
   - ☐ less than 10 minutes
   - ☐ from 10 minutes to 20 minutes
   - ☐ from 20 minutes to 30 minutes
   - ☑ more than 30 minutes

5. Overall, how satisfied were you with your experience at the clinic today?
   - ☐ extremely satisfied
   - ☑ satisfied
   - ☐ somewhat satisfied
   - ☐ unsatisfied

Comments:
I did not have an appointment so I understand why it took a long time for me to see Dr. Patton this morning.

Dr. Patton recommended I schedule my annual physical check-up next month and I followed his advice and today made an appointment for it.

Your name: _Patricia Campbell_

1. What is the purpose of this questionnaire?

    (A) To check patients' physical conditions

    (B) To encourage patients to have physical check-ups

    (C) To evaluate the effectiveness of a medicine

    (D) To measure patient satisfaction

2. What did Patricia Campbell rate the most highly?

    (A) The medical care

    (B) The office staff

    (C) The physical location

    (D) The billing process

3. What can be inferred from the questionnaire?

    (A) Dr. Patton was off duty.

    (B) The facility was renovated in 1975.

    (C) Patricia Campbell did not have an appointment.

    (D) A receptionist failed to check in Patricia Campbell.

中譯 問題 1-3：請看以下問卷。

社區診所

（自 1975 年開業至今）

[1]病患問卷

1. 今天您等了多久才看到醫生或醫療保健專家？
   - ☐ 不到 30 分鐘 　☐ 1 小時到 90 分鐘
   - ☐ 30 分鐘到 1 小時 　☑ 超過 90 分鐘

2. [2]您認為今天醫生或醫療保健專家的治療品質如何？
   - ☑ 非常好 　☐ 不滿意
   - ☐ 很好 　☐ 非常不滿意
   - ☐ 普通

3. 您認為櫃台人員或批價部門的服務品質如何？
   - ☐ 非常好 　☑ 不滿意
   - ☐ 很好 　☐ 非常不滿意
   - ☐ 普通

4. 治療結束後，您等了多久才拿到帳單？
   - ☐ 不到 10 分鐘 　☐ 20 到 30 分鐘
   - ☐ 10 到 20 分鐘 　☑ 超過 30 分鐘

5. 整體來說，您對今天看診的經驗是否滿意？
   - ☐ 非常滿意 　☐ 有點滿意
   - ☑ 滿意 　☐ 不滿意

意見：[3]我沒有預約，所以我了解為什麼今天早上要等很久才見到派頓醫生。
派頓醫生建議我下個月安排年度健康檢查，我也聽從他的建議，今天已經預約了。

姓名：*派翠西亞・坎貝爾*

單字

☐ serve 動 為…提供服務	☐ treatment 名 治療
☐ questionnaire 名 問卷	☐ unsatisfactory 形 令人不滿意的
☐ physician 名 內科醫生	☐ receptionist 名 櫃台人員，接待員
☐ specialist 名 專家	☐ annual 形 一年一次的
☐ rate 動 評價，打分數	☐ physical check-up 健康檢查

解答 **1.** (D)　**2.** (A)　**3.** (C)

1. 這份問卷的目的為何？
(A) 確認病患的身體狀況
(B) 鼓勵病患接受健康檢查
(C) 評價藥物的有效性
(D) 評估病患的滿意度

解說 注意標題　　　　　　　　（難易度）★

從標題 PATIENT QUESTIONNAIRE（病患問卷）可知是給病患填寫的問卷。從內容的 How would you rate the quality of treatment/service...?（您認為……的治療／服務品質如何？）、how satisfied were you...?（您對……是否滿意？）可知，問卷調查的是病患的滿意度，因此正確答案是 (D) To measure patient satisfaction。

2. 派翠西亞‧坎貝爾對哪一個項目評價最高？
(A) 醫療照護
(B) 辦公室員工
(C) 診所位置
(D) 批價流程

解說 注意勾選項目；問卷的題目當中，通
常有一個是正確答案　（難易度）★

從最下面的 Your name（姓名）一欄可知，填寫問卷的人是派翠西亞‧坎貝爾。五個題目中，她對第二題關於治療品質的滿意度給了 excellent（非常好）的最高評價，也就是對醫療照護感到滿意，因此正確答案是 (A) The medical care。

換句話說　正文 treatment ➡ 選項 medical care

3. 從問卷中可以推測出什麼？
(A) 派頓醫生今天沒有班。
(B) 診所曾於 1975 年進行整修。
(C) 派翠西亞‧坎貝爾沒有預約。
(D) 櫃台人員沒有幫派翠西亞‧坎貝爾掛號。

解說 問卷的意見欄通常會出現一個正確
答案　　　　　　　　　（難易度）★

對照每一個選項與問卷內容。從最後意見欄的 I did not have an appointment...（我沒有預約……）可知，派翠西亞‧坎貝爾沒有預約，因此正確答案是 (C) Patricia Campbell did not have an appointment.。

1 分鐘 CHECK!

複習「表單」的閱讀重點及 Day 2 的必背字彙。

「表單」的閱讀重點

☐ 表單包含繳費通知單、申請表、訂單、問卷、時程表、圖表、菜單等。常出現在測驗中的是公共費用的繳費通知單，以及報章雜誌的訂閱申請表。

☐ 首先從標題、表單中的詞彙來掌握表單的目的。

☐ 了解每種表單必定會出現的用詞，從表格項目找出答案。

☐ 注意寫在表格外的聯絡方式等資訊。

「表單」的必背字彙

☐ account number 帳號
☐ outstanding balance 未付清的餘款
☐ charge 名 費用
☐ due date 繳費期限
☐ payment type 繳費方式
☐ amount 名 量
☐ subscription 名 訂閱
☐ renewal 名 更新
☐ newsstand price 定價
☐ billing date 請款日

☐ period 名 期間
☐ current month 本月
☐ past due 逾期未付費用
☐ net 形 淨值的
☐ interest charge 利息費用
☐ assess 動 課以（一定費用）
☐ expire 動 到期
☐ check 名 支票
☐ questionnaire 名 問卷

Day 3

本日主題
● 文字訊息、線上對話

Day 3 | 文字訊息、線上對話

文字訊息、線上對話分成「兩人對話」和「三人（含）以上對話」兩種情況。兩個人的對話比較容易理解，三人以上的對話稍微困難，因此必須迅速掌握發文者的立場。這類文章用字口語化，字句簡短而且經常省略主詞。

STEP 1 看看這類文章的閱讀重點！

● 文字訊息

Point 1 閱讀時注意是誰、在何時、發表了什麼內容！

Point 4 從關鍵字推測公司名稱、場所或職稱！

Point 3 有時候會省略主詞！

Point 2 從前後文判斷特定語句的意思，推測發文者的想法！

閱讀時注意是誰、在何時、發表了什麼內容！

閱讀文字訊息或線上對話時，必須留意是誰、在何時、發表了什麼內容。只要從正文裡找出題目裡的主詞，通常就能夠推測出正確答案。發文者欄位中如果沒有題目裡的主詞時，請找人名。

 從前後文判斷特定語句的意思，推測發文者的想法！

有時對話中會使用像 Roger.（知道了。）這類口語的用詞。下一頁會提到，有時題目會問，發文者使用這類說法的用意何在？即使不知道該語句的意思，也可以根據前後文推測出正確答案。

 有時候會省略主詞！

有時會出現 Waiting for my luggage.（在等我的行李。）這類省略主詞的句子，習慣了就好。

 從關鍵字推測企業名稱、場所或職稱！

必須從對話中的關鍵字推測出場所或職稱，快速掌握情況。

例：attorney（律師）、contract（契約）→ lawyer's office（律師事務所）
　　prescribe medication（開處方箋）→ doctor（醫生）
　　fill the prescription（依處方箋配藥）→ pharmacist（藥劑師）

中譯

鈴木智子	下午 2:01
準時降落。你在哪裡？	
凱爾文・懷特	下午 2:02
剛走出停車場，裡面很滿，但我找到位子了。你呢？	
鈴木智子	下午 2:12
在等我的托運行李。	
凱爾文・懷特	下午 2:13
好，我們要在哪碰面？	
鈴木智子	下午 2:14
我在北航廈入境層 5 號行李轉盤這邊。你能過來嗎？	
凱爾文・懷特	下午 2:15
知道了。等我一下。	

① 與場所、職稱、公司名稱有關的題目
通常都能夠從關鍵字推測出答案。有時還會從公司名稱問產業類別。

題目

● Where are the people?（對話中的人在哪裡？）

文中的表達方式

● Landed right on time.（準時降落。）/ Carousel（行李轉盤）
答案 At an airport（在機場）

題目

● For what type of business does Mr. Smith most likely work?
（史密斯先生最有可能從事哪一類工作？）

文中的表達方式

● I am in charge of providing meals for large events.
（我負責為大型活動提供餐點。）
答案 Catering（餐飲業）

題目

● Who is Mr. Garcia?（賈西亞先生是誰？）

文中的表達方式

● Want to include the opening of the new public library as a feature story in the autumn issue.（想將新公立圖書館的開幕當做秋季號的專題報導。）
答案 A journalist（記者）

② 與特定語句有關的題目
有時題目會問，發文者使用了特定的語句，意思是什麼？這時必須從前後文判斷特定語句的意思，推測發文者的想法。

題目

● At 2:15 P.M., what does Mr. White most likely mean when he writes, "Roger"?
（下午 2 點 15 分時，懷特先生寫「Roger」最有可能是什麼意思？）

文中的表達方式

Tomoko Suzuki   2:14 P.M.

Can you make it over here?（你能過來嗎？）

Calvin White　　**2:15 P.M.**

Roger. Give me a minute.（知道了。等我一下。）

解說 下午 2 點 14 分時，鈴木智子問「你能過來嗎？」，凱爾文·懷特先是說 Roger，接著回答「等我一下。」也就是說，他待會會前往女子所在的位置，因此正確答案是 He will go to the woman's location.（他將前往女子所在的位置。）

題目

● At 11:18 A.M., what does Mr. Chen most likely mean when he writes, "I'm in"?
（上午 11 點 18 分時，陳先生寫「I'm in」最有可能是什麼意思？）

文中的表達方式

Christy White　　**11:15 A.M.**

Why don't you join our barbecue party next Sunday?
（你何不參加我們下週日的烤肉派對？）

Mike Chen　　**11:18 A.M**

I'm in. Where?（我加入。在哪裡？）

解說 只要知道 I'm in. 是「我加入 / 算我一份。」的意思，就能立刻找出正確答案。就算不知道，在 I'm in. 後面陳麥克接著問了地點，可以推測他要參加，所以正確答案是 He will participate in the barbecue party.（他將參加烤肉派對。）

加分表現

★ 與特定語句有關的題目中經常使用的口語表現

● It happens.（常有的事。）
● I'm done.（我好了。）
● I'm in.（我加入 / 算我一份。）
● Could you walk me through the steps?
（你可以一個步驟一個步驟告訴我怎麼做嗎？）
● Are you with me?（你懂我的意思嗎？）
● Got it.（知道了。）
● You bet.（當然。）

Questions 1-3 refer to the following text message chain.

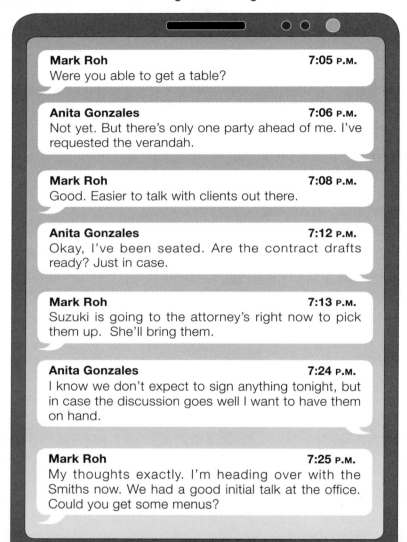

Mark Roh   7:05 P.M.
Were you able to get a table?

Anita Gonzales   7:06 P.M.
Not yet. But there's only one party ahead of me. I've requested the verandah.

Mark Roh   7:08 P.M.
Good. Easier to talk with clients out there.

Anita Gonzales   7:12 P.M.
Okay, I've been seated. Are the contract drafts ready? Just in case.

Mark Roh   7:13 P.M.
Suzuki is going to the attorney's right now to pick them up. She'll bring them.

Anita Gonzales   7:24 P.M.
I know we don't expect to sign anything tonight, but in case the discussion goes well I want to have them on hand.

Mark Roh   7:25 P.M.
My thoughts exactly. I'm heading over with the Smiths now. We had a good initial talk at the office. Could you get some menus?

1. Where is Ms. Suzuki going now?

  (A) A restaurant
  (B) A party
  (C) A law office
  (D) A corporate headquarters

2. At 7:24 P.M., what does Ms. Gonzales most likely mean when she writes, "I want to have them on hand"?

  (A) She is unsure whether Ms. Suzuki will bring the contracts.
  (B) She feels the contracts should be available if needed.
  (C) She wants to be sure the documents are safe.
  (D) She feels that the contracts are her responsibility.

3. What does Mr. Roh ask Ms. Gonzales to do?

  (A) Make a request to a server
  (B) Confirm a reservation
  (C) Set the table
  (D) Order food

中譯 問題 1-3：請看以下訊息。

馬克・盧　　　　　　晚上 7:05
有位子了嗎？

安妮塔・岡薩雷斯　　晚上 7:06
還沒，但前面只剩一組人。我已經要求要露台的位子了。

馬克・盧　　　　　　晚上 7:08
很好，那裡和客戶說話比較方便。

安妮塔・岡薩雷斯　　晚上 7:12
好，我已經在位子上坐下了。契約的草稿好了嗎？以防萬一。

馬克・盧　　　　　　晚上 7:13
[1]鈴木正要去律師那裡拿。她會帶過來。

安妮塔・岡薩雷斯　　晚上 7:24
我知道今晚不期待能簽約，但搞不好討論進行得很順利也說不定，所以[2]我想手邊要有契約。

馬克・盧　　　　　　晚上 7:25
我也是這麼想的。我現在要和史密斯他們一起過去了，我們在辦公室初步談得不錯。[3]你可以先拿菜單嗎？

單字

□ ahead of... 在…之前
□ request 動 要求
□ verandah 名 露台，走廊
□ client 名 客戶
□ contract draft 契約草稿
□ attorney 名 律師
□ head over 前往
□ initial 形 初步的

解答 1. (C) 2. (B) 3. (A)

1. 鈴木小姐正要去哪裡？
   (A) 餐廳
   (B) 派對
   (C) 律師事務所
   (D) 公司總部

解說 找出非發文者的 Suzuki

難易度 ★★★

發文者裡面沒有鈴木，因此要從訊息內容中找。馬克・盧在下午 7 點 13 分時寫 Suzuki is going to the attorney's right now...（鈴木正要去律師那裡……），也就是要去律師事務所，因此正確答案是 (C) A law office。

換句話說 正文 attorney's ➡ 選項 law office

---

2. 晚上 7 點 24 分時，岡薩雷斯小姐寫「I want to have them on hand」最有可能是什麼意思？
   (A) 她不確定鈴木小姐會不會帶契約來。
   (B) 她覺得必要時應該要能提供契約。
   (C) 她想確認文件是安全的。
   (D) 她覺得契約是她的責任。

解說 從前後文判斷特定語句的意思，推測發文者的想法

難易度 ★★

討論順利的話，很可能進展到簽約的階段，因此岡薩雷斯小姐想要確保手邊有契約，需要時就可以派上用場。也就是說，契約必須是在隨手可得的狀態，以備不時之需，所以正確答案是 (B) She feels the contracts should be available if needed.。

換句話說 正文 have them on hand ➡ 選項 available

---

3. 盧先生要岡薩雷斯小姐做什麼？
   (A) 向服務生提出要求
   (B) 確認訂位
   (C) 把餐具擺好
   (D) 點餐

解說 可從題目裡的主詞 (Roh) 的訊息推測出正確答案

難易度 ★★★

對話最後，盧先生對岡薩雷斯小姐說 Could you get some menus?（你可以先拿菜單嗎？）可以推測盧先生要她先跟服務生索取菜單，也就是向服務生提出要求，因此正確答案是 (A) Make a request to a server。

Questions 1-2 refer to the following text message chain.

Ellen Stark   3:50 P.M.
Did you drop off the travel brochures at the printer yet? How soon can they be run off?

Ali El Fundi   3:52 P.M.
Almost there. They assured me on the phone the pamphlets would take no more than 48 hours.

Ellen Stark   3:59 P.M.
Okay. Oh, Ali, we're short on legal envelopes and copier paper here at the office. Could you pick some up at a stationery shop on the way back?

Ali El Fundi   4:09 P.M.
Dropped off the printing order. Will be ready as promised. Heading to Office Depot. Anything else to get?

Ellen Stark   4:10 P.M.
Yes. After that will you have time to get some stamps at the post office? It closes at 5.

Ali El Fundi   4:12 P.M.
You bet.

---

1. When will the travel brochures most likely be ready?

(A) This evening
(B) Tomorrow morning
(C) Tomorrow afternoon
(D) The day after tomorrow

2. At 4:12 P.M., what does Mr. El Fundi most likely mean when he writes, "You bet"?

(A) He is unsure the post office will be open.
(B) He has already picked up the envelopes.
(C) He can certainly obtain the stamps.
(D) He may be short on time.

文字訊息、線上對話

中譯 問題 1-2：請看以下訊息。

艾倫・史塔克　　　　下午 3:50
你把旅遊手冊送到印刷廠了嗎？多快可以印好？

阿里・艾爾・方迪　　下午 3:52
快到了。[1]他們電話裡跟我保證冊子 48 小時內會好。

艾倫・史塔克　　　　下午 3:59
好。喔，阿里，辦公室的大信封和影印紙快沒了，你回來路上可以去文具店買一些嗎？

阿里・艾爾・方迪　　下午 4:09
印刷訂單已經下了，可以如期交貨。正要去辦公用品店，還有要買什麼嗎？

艾倫・史塔克　　　　下午 4:10
有。[2]去完文具店後你有時間去郵局買些郵票嗎？郵局五點關門。

阿里・艾爾・方迪　　下午 4:12
[2]當然。

單字

□ drop off... 把…放在特定地點
□ brochure 名 手冊
□ run off... 印刷…
□ assure 動 保證
□ pamphlet 名 小冊子

□ no more than... 不超過…
□ be short on... …不夠
□ stationery shop 文具店
□ as promised 依約
□ head to... 前往…

1. 旅遊手冊最有可能什麼時候完成？
  (A) 今天傍晚
  (B) 明天早上
  (C) 明天下午
  (D) 後天

解說 **注意對話裡的時間** （難易度）★★★

阿里‧艾爾‧方迪在下午 3 點 52 分時寫 They assured me on the phone the pamphlets would take no more than 48 hours.（他們電話裡跟我保證冊子 48 小時內會好。）也就是兩天左右，換言之大約要後天才會完成，因此正確答案是 (D) The day after tomorrow。

---

2. 下午 4 點 12 分時，艾爾‧方迪先生寫「You bet」最有可能是什麼意思？
  (A) 他不確定郵局會不會開。
  (B) 他已經拿到信封。
  (C) 他一定可以買到郵票。
  (D) 他可能沒有時間。

解說 **從前後文判斷特定語句的意思，推測發文者的想法** （難易度）★★

艾倫‧史塔克在下午 4 點 10 分問 After that will you have time to get some stamps at the post office?（去完文具店後你有時間去郵局買些郵票嗎？）艾爾‧方迪先生回答 You bet.（當然。）表示艾爾‧方迪先生可以買到郵票，因此正確答案是 (C) He can certainly obtain the stamps.。

換句話說 正文 get ➡ 選項 obtain

DAY 3

文字訊息、線上對話

時間
4分鐘

Questions 1-4 refer to the following online chat discussion.

✕

Carlo Hernandez 10:10 A.M.
Everyone report in. We've got a lot to do today.

Laurie Petrauskas 10:11 A.M.
Helen and I are still trimming the bushes in front of Sanford Investment Corp. We'll be done in about 30 minutes.

Mike Park 10:11 A.M.
Just finished raking the backyard at the Silman residence. Going to mow the lawn now. Should be done by lunch.

Leon Smith 10:12 A.M.
Just finished pruning shrubbery in front of River Tower. What's next boss?

Carlo Hernandez 10:15 A.M.
Leon, go to the Golf Estates and start the landscaping by 11:00. Laurie and Helen, please join him as soon as you can. Mike, go over there in the early afternoon when you're finished. They'll need your help.

Laurie Petrauskas 10:16 A.M.
Absolutely. We'll be there shortly.

Leon Smith 10:17 A.M.
On my way right now.

Mike Park 10:21 A.M.
I'll head over there as soon as I grab something to eat.

Lily Chang 10:21 A.M.
Sorry. Driving. Couldn't text. Stuck in traffic. On my way to do the lawn at the MacroComputing Center. Will be tied up there for the rest of the day — or at least the late afternoon.

1. Where is Ms. Petrauskas most likely working?

(A) A computer center
(B) A manufacturing plant
(C) A realtor
(D) A finance company

2. What will Mr. Park do next?

(A) Clean a lawn
(B) Cut grass
(C) Trim bushes
(D) Eat lunch

3. When will a crew likely start working at the Golf Estates?

(A) Late morning
(B) Lunchtime
(C) Early afternoon
(D) Late afternoon

4. At 10:21 A.M., what does Ms. Chang most likely mean when she writes, "Will be tied up there for the rest of the day"?

(A) She will be stuck in traffic for a long time.
(B) She will be busy most of the day.
(C) She will take a rest later today.
(D) She will not be able to text anymore today.

中譯 問題 1-4：請看以下線上對話討論。

卡洛・赫南德茲　上午 10:10
大家報告各自的情況，我們今天有很多事要做。

蘿莉・派特勞卡斯　上午 10:11
[1]海倫和我還在修剪山福德投資公司前面的灌木叢。 30 分鐘內會完成。

麥克・帕克　上午 10:11
剛耙完西爾曼住宅的後院，[2]現在要去割草坪的草。 午餐前應該會完成。

里昂・史密斯　上午 10:12
剛修剪完瑞佛塔前面的灌木叢。老闆，下個工作是什麼？

卡洛・赫南德茲　上午 10:15
[3]里昂，11 點前去高爾夫莊園做景觀美化。 蘿莉和海倫請盡快加入他。麥克，等你結束後，中午過後就過去那裡，他們會需要你的協助。

蘿莉・派特勞卡斯　上午 10:16
沒問題，我們很快就過去。

里昂・史密斯　上午 10:17
馬上過去。

麥克・帕克　上午 10:21
我吃點東西之後馬上過去。

張莉莉　上午 10:21
抱歉，正在開車，不能打字，塞在車陣中。正要去麥克羅電腦中心除草。[4]今天一整天都會忙那裡的事，至少會待到傍晚。

單字

□ trim 動 修剪
□ bush 名 灌木
□ investment 名 投資
□ corp. 名 公司（即 corporation）
□ rake 動 用耙子耙平
□ residence 名 住所，住宅
□ mow the lawn 割草坪的草
□ prune 動 修剪

□ shrubbery 名 灌木
□ estate 名 莊園
□ landscaping 名 景觀美化
□ grab 動 隨手抓取
□ text 動 發簡訊
□ (be) stuck in traffic 塞在車陣中
□ be tied up 忙碌

解答 **1.** (D) **2.** (B) **3.** (A) **4.** (B)

1. 派特勞卡斯小姐現在人最有可能在哪裡工作？
(A) 電腦中心
(B) 製造工廠
(C) 地產商
(D) 金融公司

解說 可從題目裡的主詞 (Petrauskas) 的訊息推測出正確答案 **難易度** ★★

派特勞卡斯小姐在上午 10 點 11 分寫 Helen and I are still trimming the bushes in front of Sanford Investment Corp.（海倫和我還在修剪山福德投資公司前面的灌木叢。）Investment Corp. 是投資公司，也就是說她人正在金融公司前面工作，因此正確答案是 (D) A finance company。

換句話說 **正文** Investment Corp. ➡ **選項** finance company

2. 帕克先生接下來會做什麼？
(A) 清理草坪
(B) 除草
(C) 修剪灌木叢
(D) 吃午餐

解說 可從題目裡的主詞 (Park) 的訊息推測出正確答案 **難易度** ★

帕克先生在上午 10 點 11 分寫 Going to mow the lawn now.（現在要去割草坪的草。）也就是正要去除草，因此正確答案是 (B) Cut grass。

換句話說 **正文** mow the lawn ➡ **選項** Cut grass

3. 員工有可能什麼時候開始在高爾夫莊園工作？
(A) 近中午
(B) 午餐時間
(C) 午後
(D) 傍晚

解說 找出 Golf Estates **難易度** ★★★

赫南德茲先生在上午 10 點 15 分寫 Leon, go to the Golf Estates and start the landscaping by 11:00.（里昂，11 點前去高爾夫莊園做景觀美化。）也就是說，里昂先生有可能在接近中午時開始作業，因此正確答案是 (A) Late morning。

4. 早上 10 點 21 分時，張小姐寫「Will be tied up there for the rest of the day」最有可能是什麼意思？
(A) 她會長時間塞在車陣中。
(B) 她那天大部分時間會很忙。
(C) 她今天晚一點會休息。
(D) 她今天不能再傳簡訊了。

解說 想想張莉莉在上午 10 點 21 分送出的訊息的意思，找出正確答案 **難易度** ★★

be tied up 是「忙碌」的意思，the rest of the day 是指「今天接下來的時間」，也就是說從送出訊息的現在起接下來的時間都會很忙，因此正確答案是 (B) She will be busy most of the day。

換句話說 **正文** be tied up ➡ **選項** busy
正文 for the rest of the day ➡ **選項** most of the day

1 分鐘 CHECK!

複習「文字訊息、線上對話」的閱讀重點及 Day 3 的必背字彙。

「文字訊息、線上對話」的閱讀重點

☐ 「文字訊息、線上對話」包含「兩人對話」以及「三人（含）以上的對話」。

☐ 正確答案大多在題目裡的主詞中，也就是說，閱讀時注意時間與發文者的名字，通常就能夠推測出正確答案。如果題目裡的主詞沒有出現在發文者的欄位，可在正文中找尋。

☐ 與特定語句有關的題目，可從前後文推測出正確答案。

☐ 從關鍵字或關鍵句導出場所、職稱、產業類別。

「文字訊息、線上對話」的必背字彙

☐ Roger. 知道了 / 了解了 / 收到了。
☐ Give me a minute. 等我一下 / 給我一分鐘。
☐ no more than... 不超過…
☐ as promised 依約
☐ Absolutely. 當然。
☐ text 動 發簡訊
☐ (be) stuck in traffic 塞在車陣中
☐ be tied up 忙碌

Day 4

本日主題
● 書信、電子郵件

書信和電子郵件都是 TOEIC 常考的文章類型，在多篇文章測驗中一定會出現。請先記住這類文章固有的版面格式。

閱讀書信時，除了版面格式，還要注意這封信是「誰（寄件人）」「為了什麼事（目的）」寫給「誰（收件人）」的。

STEP 1　看看這類文章的閱讀重點！

● 取消機票的書信

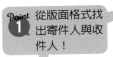

Point 1 從版面格式找出寄件人與收件人！

Rose Chung, Manager [寄件人姓名]
Oriental Imports ── [寄件人的公司名稱]
3435 San Juan Boulevard
Los Angeles, CA 90775 ── [寄件人的地址]
Tel. 310-555-2907
E-mail: rosechung@orientalimports.com
January 20 [日期]

Mark Rutgers, Agent [收件人姓名]
Eastern Dream Travel [收件人的公司名稱]
45 Palm Drive ── [收件人的地址]
Los Angeles, CA 90804
Tel. 310-555-4359

Point 2 信件的主旨寫在開頭幾行！

Point 3 注意內含慣用說法的關鍵句！

Dear Mr. Rutgers,

I am writing to you today to cancel the World Airlines ticket which you issued to me to fly from Los Angeles to Seoul on February 2nd. I regret to inform you that due to some staff changes here in our office I will not be able to make the trip.
[慣用說法（表示要求）]
Could you kindly refund my payment by sending me a check for the balance? I understand that I may not receive a full refund since the ticket has already been issued.
[慣用說法（表示要求）]
I would like to ask you to keep my personal information on file (my name, address, etc.) as I will be re-booking the flight later this year.

Thank you for your help in this matter.

Sincerely yours,
Rose Chung [署名]
Rose Chung
Manager ── [職稱]
Encl.: copy of e-ticket [附件]

1 從版面格式找出寄件人與收件人的關係!

商業書信的格式,通常在信件中央上方或右上角印有公司名稱(寄件人姓名)、地址、聯絡方式等,下方則是寄件日期、收件人姓名、地址、聯絡方式等。在正文最後的左下角則有署名、職稱等。版面的格式很固定,公司名稱與職稱都是了解信件主旨的重要提示。

閱讀電子郵件時則要注意 To(收件人)、From(寄件人)、Re(回覆)、Subject(主旨)、Date(寄件日期)等欄位。有時在寄件人的署名最下面還會有附加檔案(Enclosure/Encl.)。

2 信件主旨通常寫在開頭兩、三行!

書信、電子郵件多半在開頭幾行就會寫出與主旨有關的內容及後續細節。

3 注意內含慣用說法的關鍵句!

書信、電子郵件經常使用慣用說法,因此請牢記表示目的、要求等的關鍵句。

經理 鍾蘿絲
東方進口公司
洛杉磯 CA 90775
山黃大道 3435 號
電話:310-555-2907
電子郵件:rosechung@orientalimports.com
1 月 20 日

代理人 馬克・魯特格斯
東方夢旅遊公司
洛杉磯 CA 90804
棕櫚路 45 號
電話:310-555-4359

親愛的魯特格斯先生:

今天這封信是要取消你幫我訂的、2 月 2 日世界航空從洛杉磯飛往首爾的機票。很遺憾要通知你,因為我們辦公室的人事異動,我這趟旅行無法成行了。

退款的餘額能不能請你用支票退回給我呢?我知道我可能無法收到全額退款,因為機票已經開票了。

我想請你將我的個人資料(姓名、地址等)存檔,因為今年晚一點我會重新訂票。

謝謝你在這件事上的協助。

經理

鍾蘿絲

鍾蘿絲

敬上

附件：電子機票副本

---

1 與書信、電子郵件的目的有關的題目
書信、電子郵件的目的常以慣用說法來描述。從這裡可找出書信與電子郵件的目的。

題目

● What is the main purpose of the letter?（這封信的主要目的為何？）

文中的表達方式

● **感謝** I am writing to express my gratitude.（這封信是為了表達我的感謝。）

● **通知** I am pleased to inform you about our cultural festival.
（很高興通知你關於文化節的事。）

● **聯絡** I am contacting you to cancel my reservation for next week.
（這封信是為了取消我下週的預約。）

● **詢問** We would like to inquire about your special sale.
（我們想詢問有關特賣的事。）

● **邀請** We would like to invite you to make a presentation at our annual
marketing conference.
（我們想邀請你在我們的年度行銷會議上發表演說。）

● **確認** This letter confirms your registration for the marketing seminar.
（這封信用來確認你已經報名參加行銷講座。）

● **客訴** I regret to inform you that I was billed twice.
（很遺憾通知你我被收取了兩次費用。）

● **道歉** We are sorry for having billed you twice by mistake.
（很抱歉我們不小心收了你兩次費用。）

● **回覆** I am writing in response to your letter of October 2nd.
（這封信是為了回覆你於 10 月 2 日的來信。）

● **具體說明原因** I am writing to you because my credit card is not working well.
（我寫這封信是因為我的信用卡無法正常使用。）

2 與具體的要求有關的題目

書信、電子郵件的題目經常會問收件人的要求為何。在信件中後段通常可以找到以下用來表示要求的關鍵句。

題目

- What does A ask B to do?（A 要求 B 做什麼？）
- What is B asked to do?（B 被要求做什麼？）

文中的表達方式

- Please complete our customer satisfaction survey.
  （請完成我們的顧客滿意度調查。）
- Could you kindly refund my payment?
  （你可以退回我所支付的款項嗎？）
- Would you please dispose of your old credit card?
  （可以請你銷毀你舊的信用卡嗎？）
- Would it be possible to take a tour of some of your properties on Monday April 16?（4 月 16 日星期一能不能去參觀一下你們幾個物件？）
- I would like to ask you to keep my personal information on file.
  （我想請你將我的個人資料存檔。）
- He would like you to send him an estimate for bulk buying by e-mail order.
  （他想請你將透過電子郵件大量訂購的估價單寄給他。）
- I would appreciate it if you could arrange a time to...
  （如果你可以安排時間做……我會很感激的。）

加分表現

★ 書信與電子郵件常用字彙

- attach 動 附加
- enclose 動 隨信附上
- subject 名 主旨
- be forwarded to... 轉寄給…
- respond 動 回應
- state 動 說，表示
- confirm 動 確認
- refer to... 參考…
- regarding/concerning / in regard to / with regard to... 關於…

- attachment 名 附加檔案
- enclosure 名 附件
- inquiry about... 有關…的詢問
- in response to... 回應…
- reply to... 回覆…
- inform 動 通知
- remind 動 提醒
- with reference to... 關於…

Questions 1-3 refer to the following e-mail.

TO:	Richard Sanford <rsanford@comstock.com>
FROM:	Mary Salazar <msalazar@bus.net>
SUB:	Your participation in the marketing seminar
DATE:	March 15

Dear Mr. Sanford:

I am pleased to inform you that we will be holding our annual Business Education Forum, as scheduled, from May 1 to May 4 at the River Convention Center. This e-mail confirms your registration for the "Internet Opportunities in Retail Marketing" seminar by Adolph Sampson on Saturday May 2, from 1 to 5 P.M.

To maximize participation, we limit enrollment in each seminar to 10 business professionals. We kindly request that if you, as sales director, would like to register any of your staff in this year's seminars, you do so as soon as possible.

Thank you for joining us.

Mary S.
Event Coordinator

P.S. I am attaching to this e-mail the brochure of our programs for the conference. You can also access this information at www.businessed.com.

1. What is the main purpose of this e-mail?

    (A) To announce a schedule change
    (B) To request a registration fee
    (C) To confirm enrollment
    (D) To publicize new programs

2. Who is Mr. Sanford?

    (A) A sales director
    (B) A conference presenter
    (C) An internet marketer
    (D) An event coordinator

3. What is included with this e-mail?

    (A) A payment form
    (B) A conference pamphlet
    (C) A map of the convention center
    (D) A list of local accommodations

中譯 問題 1-3：請看以下電子郵件。

收件人：理查‧山福德 <rsanford@comstock.com>
寄件人：瑪麗‧撒拉札 <msalazar@bus.net>
主旨：參加行銷講座
日期：3 月 15 日

親愛的山福德先生：

很高興通知您，我們將如期於 5 月 1 日至 5 月 4 日於瑞佛會議中心舉辦年度商業教育論壇。[1]這封電子郵件用來確認您已經報名 5 月 2 日週六下午 1 點到 5 點由安道夫‧山普森主講的「零售行銷的網路機會」講座。

為了盡可能提高參與度，我們限制每個講座僅能有 10 名商業界的專業人士參加。若[2]業務總監您想為員工報名今年的講座，我們懇請您盡快報名。

謝謝您的參與。

活動主辦人
瑪麗‧撒拉札

附註：[3]隨信附上會議的活動手冊。您也可以到 www.businessed.com 了解相關資訊。

單字

□ participation 名 參加，參與
□ seminar 名 研討會，講座
□ hold 動 舉辦
□ forum 名 論壇
□ registration 名 報名，登記
□ retail 形 零售的

□ maximize 動 使最大化
□ enrollment 名 報名參加人數
□ professional 名 專業人士
□ staff 名 職員，工作人員
□ coordinator 名 協調者
□ access 動 取得（資料等）

解答 **1.** (C)　**2.** (A)　**3.** (B)

1. 這封電子郵件的主要目的為何？
(A) 宣布行程變更
(B) 索取報名費
(C) 確認報名
(D) 宣傳新的課程

解說 注意開頭兩、三行和表示確認的關鍵句 （難易度）★

電子郵件的主旨一定會出現在開頭幾行。從第一段第二句的 This e-mail confirms your registration...（這封電子郵件用來確認您已經報名……）可知，郵件的目的是確認報名，因此正確答案是 (C) To confirm enrollment。

換句話說 |正文| registration ➡ |選項| enrollment

2. 山福德先生是誰？
(A) 業務總監
(B) 會議講者
(C) 網路行銷人
(D) 活動主辦人

解說 從 To 找出收件人 （難易度）★

收件人是山福德先生，可知第二段第二句 We kindly request that if you, as sales director, would like to...（若業務總監您……我們懇請您……）的 you 指的是業務總監山福德先生，因此正確答案是 (A) A sales director。小心別與講者山普森搞混了。

3. 這封電子郵件附加了什麼？
(A) 付款表格
(B) 會議手冊
(C) 會議中心的地圖
(D) 當地住宿地點的清單

解說 注意 P.S. （難易度）★

P.S.（附註）的部分提到了附加檔案。從 I am attaching to this e-mail the brochure of our programs for the conference.（隨信附上會議的活動手冊。）可知，附上的是會議手冊，因此正確答案是 (B) A conference pamphlet。

換句話說 |正文| the brochure of our programs for the conference ➡ |選項| A conference pamphlet

Questions 1-3 refer to the following letter.

ATLANTIC AIR

125 Market Street
New York

October 15th

Dear Ms. Parker:

I am writing in response to your letter of October 2nd in which you stated that on September 1st we double charged you for the tickets you purchased for your September 14th Boston-Los Angeles flight. After checking with our accounting department, I would like to sincerely apologize for having billed you twice. Apparently, we were experiencing some problems with our Web site at that time.

I have refunded your credit card in full for the amount you were overcharged in error. I am also enclosing with this letter a $100 certificate that you can use toward the purchase of future tickets on Atlantic Air. Let me say again we regret the error and are grateful to you for bringing it to our attention.

Sincerely yours,

Carl Wundt

Vice President, Customer Service
P.S. Please note the certificate is non-transferable and must be used within one year of the date of issue.

1. When did the customer report a problem?

(A) September 1st
(B) September 14th
(C) October 2nd
(D) October 15th

2. Why was this letter sent to Ms. Parker?

(A) To offer a sales promotion
(B) To confirm a reservation
(C) To apologize for an error
(D) To make a complaint

3. What is NOT true of Atlantic Air's response to Ms. Parker's letter?

(A) It rescheduled a flight.
(B) It refunded a payment.
(C) It explained the cause of a problem.
(D) It provided a money-saving coupon.

中譯 問題 1-3：請看以下信件。

大西洋航空
紐約市場街 125 號

10 月 15 日

親愛的帕克小姐：

[1]這封信是為了回覆您於 10 月 2 日的來信，信中您提到 9 月 1 日我們重複收取了您所購買、於 9 月 14 日從波士頓飛往洛杉磯的機票費用。與會計部門確認後，[2]我想誠心地為重複收費一事向您致歉。顯然[3]當時我們的網站出了一些問題。

[3]我已經將不小心溢收的費用全額退還到您的信用卡裡。隨信並附上 100 美元折價券，下次您購買大西洋航空的機票時可以使用。請容我再度對這次的錯誤向您致歉，並感謝您的提醒。

客服部副理
卡爾・馮特

敬上
附註：請注意折價券不可轉讓，且必須於發行日起一年內使用完畢。

單字
- □ double charge 重複收費
- □ purchase 動 購買
- □ apologize for... 為…而道歉
- □ bill 動 要…付款
- □ refund 動 退費
- □ overcharge 動 超收費用
- □ certificate 名 折價券
- □ regret 動 懊悔，感到遺憾
- □ grateful 形 感謝的
- □ non-transferable 形 不可轉讓的

解答 **1.** (C) **2.** (C) **3.** (A)

1. 顧客什麼時候提出問題？

(A) 9 月 1 日

(B) 9 月 14 日

(C) 10 月 2 日

(D) 10 月 15 日

解說 找出寄件日期；注意表示回覆的關鍵句

難易度 ★

從第一段第一句的 I am writing in response to your letter of October 2nd...（這封信是為了回覆您於 10 月 2 日的來信……）可知，顧客於 10 月 2 日去信提出問題，因此正確答案是 (C) October 2nd。

2. 這封信為什麼會寄給帕克小姐？

(A) 提供促銷活動

(B) 確認預約

(C) 為錯誤道歉

(D) 提出客訴

解說 注意開頭兩、三行和表示道歉的關鍵句

難易度 ★

從第一段第二句的 I would like to sincerely apologize for having billed you twice.（我想誠心地為重複收費一事向您致歉。）可知，這封信的目的是為了錯誤而道歉，因此正確答案是 (C) To apologize for an error。

換句話說 **正文** having billed you twice ➡ **選項** an error

3. 關於大西洋航空對帕克小姐信件的回覆，何者為非？

(A) 更改了航班時間。

(B) 退回了款項。

(C) 解釋了問題發生的原因。

(D) 提供了省錢的折價券。

解說 NOT 問句通常可用消去法解題

難易度 ★

第一段最後一句的 we were experiencing some problems with our Web site at that time（當時我們的網站出了一些問題）說明問題的原因，第二段的 I have refunded...（我已經將費用退還……）說明已退款，I am also enclosing with this letter a $100 certificate...（隨信並附上 100 美元折價券……）說明提供折價券，分別與選項 (C)、(B)、(D) 相符。信中沒有提到更改航班時間，因此正確答案是 (A) It rescheduled a flight.。

Questions 1-3 refer to the following e-mail.

To: Mark Kurzweiler <mkurzweiler@metroproperty.com>

From: Leslie Adams <leslieadams@comcast.biz>

Date: April 10th

Dear Mr. Kurzweiler,

I have been reviewing the Greenfield City apartments featured on your company's Metro Property Web site and would like to arrange a time to see them firsthand.

Last week I accepted a position as a legal assistant at a law firm in Greenfield City. I will begin working at Thomson and Roberts Ltd. at the beginning of next month and plan to move my belongings on April 27.

Would it be possible to take a tour of some of your apartments and residences on Monday April 16th? I am interested in signing a one-year lease for a two-bedroom unit.

Kindly contact me by cell phone (435-555-6783). If I cannot answer at that time, please leave a message.

You have my permission to check my credit rating.

Leslie Adams

1. Why did Leslie Adams contact Mark Kurzweiler?

(A) To apply for a position
(B) To ask that he show her some properties
(C) To arrange for a moving company
(D) To request some legal assistance

2. What is stated about Ms. Adams?

(A) She would like to purchase a house.
(B) She designed her company's Web site.
(C) She has previously lived in Greenfield.
(D) She will start a new job in May.

3. When will Leslie Adams probably meet Mark Kurzweiler?

(A) April 10th
(B) April 16th
(C) April 27th
(D) May 1st

中譯 問題 1-3：請看以下電子郵件。

收件人：馬克‧克魯威勒 <mkurzweiler@metroproperty.com>
寄件人：蕾斯莉‧亞當斯 <leslieadams@comcast.biz>
日期：4 月 10 日

親愛的克魯威勒先生：

我最近在看貴公司都會地產網站上格林菲爾德市的公寓，¹想安排時間親自去看看。

上週我接受了格林菲爾德市某家律師事務所的法務助理一職，²下個月初就會開始在湯森與羅伯茨公司工作，並計畫於 4 月 27 日將我的行李搬過去。

³4 月 16 日星期一能不能去參觀一下你們一些公寓和住房？我想找兩房的房子，簽一年租約。

請以行動電話 (435-555-6783) 與我聯絡。若我未能及時接聽，請留言。

您可以查看我的信用評等。

蕾斯莉‧亞當斯

單字

□ review 動 檢閱，檢討
□ property 名 房產，地產
□ firsthand 副 直接
□ position 名 職位，職務
□ legal assistant 法務助理

□ belongings 名 所有物
□ take a tour of... 參觀…
□ lease 名 租約
□ permission 名 許可
□ credit rating 信用評等

解答 **1.** (B)　**2.** (D)　**3.** (B)

1. 蕾斯莉·亞當斯為什麼要聯絡馬克·克魯威勒？
(A) 為了應徵職缺
(B) 為了請他帶她看一些房子
(C) 為了安排搬家公司
(D) 為了要求法律協助

解說 注意表示要求的關鍵句　（難易度）★

從第一段的 I have been reviewing the Greenfield City apartments ... and would like to arrange a time to see them firsthand.（我最近在看格林菲爾德市的公寓⋯⋯想安排時間親自去看看。）可知，蕾斯莉想參觀克魯威勒的公司仲介的公寓，也就是要他帶她去看房子，因此正確答案是 (B) To ask that he show her some properties。

換句話說 正文 apartments ➡ 選項 properties

2. 信中關於亞當斯小姐有何敘述？
(A) 她想買房子。
(B) 她設計她公司的網站。
(C) 她過去曾住在格林菲爾德。
(D) 她將於五月開始新工作。

解說 從 Date 找出寄件日期　（難易度）★★

信是 4 月 10 日寄的。從第二段最後的 I will begin working at Thomson and Roberts Ltd. at the beginning of next month...（下個月初就會開始在湯森與羅伯茨公司工作⋯⋯）可知，亞當斯小姐將於下個月開始新工作，也就是五月，因此正確答案是 (D) She will start a new job in May.。

換句話說 正文 begin working ➡ 選項 start a new job

3. 蕾斯莉·亞當斯可能於何時和馬克·克魯威勒碰面？
(A) 4 月 10 日
(B) 4 月 16 日
(C) 4 月 27 日
(D) 5 月 1 日

解說 找出日期；注意表示要求的關鍵句

（難易度）★

從第三段的 Would it be possible to take a tour of some of your apartments and residences on Monday April 16th?（4 月 16 日星期一能不能去參觀一下你們一些公寓和住房？）可知，蕾斯莉希望在 4 月 16 日看房子，因此正確答案是 (B) April 16th。

1 分鐘 CHECK!

複習「書信、電子郵件」的閱讀重點及 Day 4 的必背字彙。

「書信、電子郵件」的閱讀重點

☐ 書信、電子郵件是多篇文章測驗的必考題型，閱讀時請注意版面格式。

☐ 書信的話，通常在中央上方或右上角有寄件人姓名、公司名稱、地址等，下方則是寄件日期、收件人姓名、地址等。

☐ 電子郵件的話，To 是收件人，From 是寄件人，Re 是回覆，Subject 是主旨，Date 則是寄件日期。

☐ 主旨通常寫在開頭兩、三行，理解主旨之後再閱讀正文。

☐ 注意內含慣用說法的關鍵句。

「書信、電子郵件」的必背字彙

☐ inform 動 通知
☐ refund 動 退費
☐ confirm 動 確認
☐ in response to... 回應…
☐ attach 動 附加
☐ attachment 名 附加檔案
☐ enclose 動 隨信附上
☐ enclosure 名 附件
☐ inquiry about... 有關…的詢問
☐ be forwarded to... 轉寄給…
☐ remind 動 提醒

Day 5

本日主題

● 通知、公告、企業內部公告

通知與公告是對多數人宣布、發表特定事項的文章，最常出現在測驗中的是公共設施規則的變更、活動通知等。企業內部公告則是寫給公司員工看的文章，內容多半與人事異動、公司內部規則變更、設施改裝等有關。

和之前介紹過的廣告一樣，閱讀通知時必須找出這是「誰（發布者）」對「誰（對象）」通知「什麼事情」。

STEP 1 看看這類文章的閱讀重點！

● 收垃圾日的變更通知

Point **1** 注意標題與粗體字！

通知的目的 ## Albion Town Garbage Removal

Notice: Change in Collection Schedule Effective May 1st

Due to the introduction of new collection routes, our garbage pick-up days are changing. Please carefully note the new days and adjust your disposal timetable accordingly.

Point **3** 從內含慣用說法的關鍵句推測出指示內容！

> New Collection Day for Burnable Trash: Mondays & Fridays
> New Collection Day for Non-Burnable Trash: Wednesdays
> New Collection Day for Newspaper Recycling: Tuesdays
> New Collection Day for Bottles & Cans: Thursdays

慣用說法

Point **2** 注意條列式內容！

Remember to place your solid waste immediately outside your residence in only those trash containers approved by our Albion town council.

Point **4** 注意星號 (*) 與最後的資訊！

*Anyone disposing of non-burnable trash together with burnable trash will be subject to a $100 fine.
*New collection routes and schedules go into effect May 1st.

Any questions should be directed to the Albion Town Waste Management Office by calling (066) 555-4473.

從標題與粗體字掌握目的和對象！

注意閱讀標題與粗體字的內容，從這裡大多能推測出通知的目的與對象。沒有標題的話，請注意正文開頭的部分。

 詳細規則、變更的內容以條列方式表示！

日期、星期、場所等的詳細規則多半以簡單明瞭的條列方式書寫。

 從內含慣用說法的關鍵句推測出指示內容！

通知常會出現 would like to announce that...（在此宣布…）、remember to...（請記得…）、bring your attention to...（請你注意…）、Please notice...（請注意…）等慣用說法，透過這些關鍵句可得知重要的指示內容。

 注意 Note、星號 (*) 和最後的資訊！

洽詢方式、注意事項、補充資訊等通常寫在 Note 或通知的最後。

中譯

艾比昂市垃圾清運

注意：清運時間變更自 5 月 1 日起生效

因為採用新的清運路線，我們的垃圾清運日即將變更。請仔細注意新的日期，並依此調整您的垃圾清理時間表。

> 可燃垃圾的新清運日：週一及週五
> 不可燃垃圾的新清運日：週三
> 報紙回收的新清運日：週二
> 瓶罐的新清運日：週四

請記得將固體廢棄物直接放置在屋外的垃圾容器中，且必須使用經艾比昂市議會認可的容器。

* 將不可燃與可燃垃圾混合丟棄者，將處以 100 美元罰款。
* 新的清運路線及時間表自 5 月 1 日起生效。

若有任何問題，請聯絡艾比昂市廢棄物管理局，電話：(066) 555-4473。

1 與通知的目的有關的題目
通知的目的多半寫在標題，如果沒有，請找表示通知的關鍵句。

題目

- What is the main purpose of the notice/memo?
  （這份通知／備忘錄的主要目的為何？）

文中的表達方式

- The Transit Authority would like to announce an increase in the cost of both individual tickets and monthly passes.（運輸局在此宣布調漲普通票和月票票價。）
- Please be advised that our garbage pick-up day will be changed effective May 1st.（請注意我們的垃圾清運日即將變更，並自 5 月 1 日起生效。）
- Remember to separate burnable trash from non-burnable trash.
  （請記得將可燃垃圾和不可燃垃圾分開。）
- Please note that our business hours are from 9:00 A.M. to 7:00 P.M. on Mondays.（請注意我們週一的營業時間自早上 9 點至晚上 7 點。）
- We also want to bring your attention to the fact that during construction, service in the main elevator in the manufacturing facility will be suspended.
  （我們也想請大家注意，在施工期間，製造工廠的主要電梯將暫時停止運作。）
- We want to alert you to the fact that the renovation of the company cafeteria will begin in mid-January.
  （我們想提醒大家，公司餐廳的整修工程將於一月中開始。）
- We would like to draw your attention to the fact that there have been changes to the expense reporting procedures.
  （我們希望大家注意，經費核銷的程序有所變更。）
- We would like to remind you to carefully organize the documents.
  （我們想提醒大家小心整理文件。）

2 與實施日期有關的題目
通知內容的實施日期（如：何時開始執行，何時截止等）和實施期間可能造成的影響很常考。

題目

- When will it go into effect?（什麼時候開始生效？）

- Notice: Change in Collection Schedule Effective May 1st
  （注意：清運時間變更自 5 月 1 日起生效）
- Effective date: From July 1（生效日：自 7 月 1 日起）

3 與洽詢方式有關的題目

與其他類型的文章一樣，問到洽詢方式時，請看通知的最後。

題目

- According to the notice, who can answer questions?
  （根據通知內容，誰能回答問題？）

文中的表達方式

- If you have any questions about the new parking lot, please direct them to any member of the security staff.
  （如果你對新的停車場有任何疑問，請詢問任何一位保全員。）
- You can reach David Chen at davidenchen@santos.com or by calling 123-4653 ext. 534.（想找陳大衛，可以寫信到 davidenchen@santos.com，或撥打電話 123-4653，分機 534。）

加分表現

★ 出現在通知裡的慣用說法

- would like to announce that...（在此宣布…）
- Please be advised that...（請注意……）
- Remember to...（請記得……）
- Please note that...（請注意……）
- bring your attention to...（請你注意…）
- We want to alert you to the fact that...（我們想提醒你……）
- draw your attention to...（請你注意…）
- remind you to...（提醒你要…）

Questions 1-3 refer to the following announcement.

CAFETERIA RENOVATION ANNOUNCEMENT

February 5th

The employee cafeteria on the 3rd floor of the manufacturing plant will be closed from February 15th to May 31st.

All workers should use the executive dining hall in the Headquarters Building. Meal times and meal prices will remain the same.

We also want to bring your attention to the fact that during construction, service in the main elevator in the manufacturing plant will be suspended. However, the freight elevator on the south end will continue to operate but should be used only for construction materials. All personnel are to use the stairs at all times.

If you have any questions about the status of the cafeteria or use of elevators or stairs, please direct your questions to any member of the security staff.

1. What is the main purpose of the notice?

(A) To broadcast an important security alert
(B) To publicize the opening of a new building
(C) To report a proposed change in menu
(D) To announce the temporary closing of a facility

2. What is unavailable for use during the construction period?

(A) The employee coffee shop
(B) The lobby of the Headquarters Building
(C) The elevator in the production facility
(D) The executive dining hall

3. According to the notice, who can answer questions?

(A) Cafeteria staff
(B) Company guards
(C) Company executives
(D) Construction workers

中譯 問題 1-3：請看以下公告。

員工餐廳整修公告
2 月 5 日

製造工廠三樓的[1]員工餐廳自 2 月 15 日起至 5 月 31 日止將停止營業。

所有員工可以使用總部大樓的主管專用餐廳，供餐時間及餐點價格將維持不變。

我們也想請大家注意，[2]在施工期間，製造工廠的主要電梯將暫時停止運作。不過，南端的貨梯會繼續運作，但僅用於運送建材。所有人員請一律使用樓梯。

如果你對餐廳的狀況或電梯、樓梯的使用有任何疑問，[3]請詢問任何一位保全員。

單字

- □ renovation 名 整修，改裝
- □ headquarters 名 總部
- □ remain the same 維持不變
- □ construction 名 建設，施工
- □ suspend 動 暫時停止
- □ freight 名 貨物
- □ operate 動 運作
- □ construction material 建材
- □ stair 名 樓梯
- □ status 名 狀況，情況
- □ direct 動 將…轉給某人
- □ security staff 保全員

1. (D) **2.** (C) **3.** (B)

1. 這份通知的主要目的為何？
  (A) 公告一項重要的安全警告
  (B) 公開新大樓的開幕
  (C) 報告更換菜單的提案
  (D) 宣布某個設施暫時關閉

解說　注意開頭部分　　難易度 ★

從通知第一段的 The employee cafeteria ... will be closed from February 15th to May 31st.（員工餐廳自 2 月 15 日起至 5 月 31 日止將停止營業。）可知，員工餐廳在特定期間不營業，也就是通知某個設施暫時關閉，因此正確答案是 (D) To announce the temporary closing of a facility。

換句話說　正文 be closed from February 15th to May 31st
  ➡ 選項 temporary closing
  正文 employee cafeteria ➡ 選項 facility

2. 在施工期間，無法使用什麼？
  (A) 員工咖啡廳
  (B) 總部大樓的大廳
  (C) 製造工廠的電梯
  (D) 主管專用餐廳

解說　注意表示通知的關鍵句和各段落的開頭　　難易度 ★★★

施工期間無法使用的設施，寫在表示通知的關鍵句裡。從第三段的 We also want to bring your attention to the fact that during construction, service in the main elevator in the manufacturing plant will be suspended.（我們也想請大家注意，在施工期間，製造工廠的主要電梯將暫時停止運作。）可知，製造工廠的電梯無法使用，因此正確答案是 (C) The elevator in the production facility。

換句話說　正文 manufacturing plant ➡ 選項 production facility

3. 根據通知內容，誰能回答問題？
  (A) 餐廳員工
  (B) 公司警衛
  (C) 公司主管
  (D) 建築工人

解說　注意最後的洽詢方式　　難易度 ★

從最後一句 If you have any questions..., please direct your questions to any member of the security staff.（如果你……有任何疑問，請詢問任何一位保全員。）可知，有問題可以問保全員，也就是公司警衛，因此正確答案是 (B) Company guards。

換句話說　正文 security staff ➡ 選項 Company guards

Questions 1-4 refer to the following notice.

NOTICE

Increase in Bus Fares

Service Areas: Central City, North Suburbs, South Suburbs
Effective date: From July 1

The Transit Authority would like to announce an increase in the cost of both individual tickets and monthly passes for three service areas. —[1]—. The cost of a single ticket will rise from $1.80 to $2.00, and a monthly pass in the Metro area will increase from $25 to $30.

We would like to bring your attention to the fact that there will be no changes in bus timetables or in routes. —[2]—. As before, bus drivers will continue to provide you, upon request, with route and timetable information. —[3]—.

Be advised that passengers boarding a bus without paying the proper fare will be subject to a $250 penalty fee. —[4]—.

1. What is the purpose of the notice?

(A) To announce a change in bus routes
(B) To report a change in bus schedules
(C) To introduce changes in bus fares
(D) To publicize a change in bus service areas

2. What can be inferred from the notice?

(A) The Central City area is unaffected by the change.
(B) The announced changes will take effect on July 1st.
(C) Bus drivers are unable to provide fare information.
(D) Bus schedules in the city and suburbs will be changed.

3. According to the notice, what might happen if passengers board the bus without a ticket?

(A) They will have to stand.
(B) They will have to pay a fine.
(C) They will lose their passes.
(D) They will have to leave the bus.

4. In which of the positions marked [1], [2], [3], and [4] does the following sentence best belong?

"However, as a matter of policy, they do not provide change."

(A) [1]
(B) [2]
(C) [3]
(D) [4]

中譯 問題 1-4：請看以下通知。

通知
¹公車票價調漲

服務區域：市中央區、北郊區、南郊區
²生效日：自 7 月 1 日起

運輸局在此¹宣布調漲三個區域的普通票和月票票價。—[1]—。單程票將從 1.80 美元調漲為 2.00 美元，市區月票則從 25 美元調漲為 30 美元。

我們想請您注意，公車時刻表或公車路線不會有任何變動。—[2]—。和以往一樣，若您提出要求，⁴公車司機將會繼續為您提供路線及時刻表資訊。—[3]—。

注意，³未支付適當車資的乘客將處以 250 美元罰款。—[4]—。

單字

□ bus fare 公車票價
□ effective date 生效日
□ transit 名 運輸
□ monthly pass 月票
□ single ticket 單程票
□ timetable 名 時刻表

□ route 名 路線
□ upon request 一經要求
□ board 動 上（車、船、飛機等交通工具）
□ proper 形 適當的
□ be subject to... 受⋯的約束
□ penalty fee 罰款

1. 這份通知的目的是什麼？
(A) 宣布公車路線的變更
(B) 報告公車時刻表的變更
(C) 介紹公車票價的變更
(D) 公開公車服務區域的變更

解說 注意標題、粗體字、開頭部分

難易度 ★

從標題的 Increase in Bus Fares（公車票價調漲）可知，通知的目的在公告公車票價調漲，也就是告知公車票價變更，因此正確答案是 (C) To introduce changes in bus fares。也可以從第一段的 announce an increase in the cost of both individual tickets and monthly passes（宣布調漲普通票和月票票價）來判斷。

換句話說 正文 Increase ➡ 選項 changes

2. 從通知中可以推測出什麼？
(A) 市中央區未受這次變更影響。
(B) 公告的變更將自 7 月 1 日起生效。
(C) 公車司機無法提供票價資訊。
(D) 市區及郊區的公車時刻表將有所變更。

解說 看清楚各個項目，生效日很常考

難易度 ★★★

從 Effective date（生效日）可知，從 7 月 1 日起開始生效，因此正確答案是 (B) The announced changes will take effect on July 1st.。市中央區在調漲範圍內，且文中沒有提到時刻表變更，所以不選 (A)、(D)。(C) 無法從文章內容推斷，所以不選。

3. 根據通知內容，如果乘客搭車沒買票，可能會發生什麼事？
(A) 他們必須站著。
(B) 他們必須付罰款。
(C) 他們會失去月票。
(D) 他們必須下車。

解說 注意最後一句和表示通知的關鍵句

難易度 ★★

從最後一段的 will be subject to a $250 penalty fee（將處以 250 美元罰款）可知，不依規定支付車資的乘客將處以罰款，因此正確答案是 (B) They will have to pay a fine.。

換句話說 正文 penalty fee ➡ 選項 fine

4. 下列句子最適合放在 [1]、[2]、[3]、[4] 哪一個位置？
「然而，依據政策規定，他們不提供找零。」
(A) [1]
(B) [2]
(C) [3]
(D) [4]

解說 插入句的題目要注意連接詞、副詞

難易度 ★★★

插入句一開始是表示轉折的連接詞 However，表示插入句必須是前述內容的轉折。如果將句子放在「司機會繼續提供路線及時刻表資訊」後面，意思會變成「司機會提供資訊，但是不找零」，合乎邏輯，因此正確答案是 (C) [3]。插入句的 they 指的就是 bus drivers。

DAY 5
通知、公告、企業內部公告

Questions 1-3 refer to the following notice.

ANNOUNCEMENT: ANNUAL CHARITY EVENT

Sponsored by the Mayfield Public Schools
Parent Teacher Association

Date	**Wednesday, August 10**
Time	**1:00 P.M. - 5:00 P.M.**
Location	**Lake Park**
City/Town	**Mayfield**

Description
Please join us for a wonderful afternoon of fun.

The family-friendly event includes:
– Full buffet and barbecue
– Live music and dancing
– Prizes
– Face painting, pony rides, magicians, and much more ...

Tickets
Adults ···································· $30, includes full buffet
Senior Citizens ····················· $20, includes full buffet
Young Adults (ages 13-20) ······· $25, includes full buffet,
                                          and prize drawing
Children (ages 12 and under) ···· $15, includes full buffet,
                                          and prize drawing

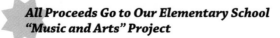
All Proceeds Go to Our Elementary School
"Music and Arts" Project

1. For whom is the notice mainly intended?

    (A) Public officials
    (B) Local families
    (C) School board members
    (D) Retired workers

2. What is NOT true about the charity event?

    (A) It will be held in the afternoon.
    (B) It features a musical performance.
    (C) It is free for young children.
    (D) It includes drawings for prizes.

3. What project will benefit from the event?

    (A) A dance theater
    (B) A senior citizen association
    (C) A new school construction
    (D) A music and arts program

中譯 問題 1-3：請看以下通知。

公告：年度慈善活動
由梅菲德公立學校[1]家長教師會主辦

日期：8 月 10 日星期三
時間：下午 1 點至 5 點
地點：湖濱公園
城市 / 城鎮：梅菲德

詳細內容
請和我們共享美好愉快的午後。

[1]家庭活動包含：
– 全套自助餐和烤肉
– 現場音樂和舞蹈表演
– 各式獎品
– 臉部彩繪、騎小馬、魔術表演等等……

票價
成人 …………………………………30 美元，含全套自助餐
年長者………………………………20 美元，含全套自助餐
青少年（13-20 歲）………………25 美元，含全套自助餐及抽獎
[2]兒童（12 歲〔含〕以下）………15 美元，含全套自助餐及抽獎

[3]所有收入將捐給我們國小的「音樂與藝術」計畫

單字

☐ charity 名 慈善
☐ sponsor 動 主辦
☐ association 名 協會

☐ description 名 說明，詳細內容
☐ prize drawing 抽獎
☐ proceeds 名 收益

1. 這份通知的主要對象是誰？
(A) 公務員
(B) 當地的家庭
(C) 學校委員會成員
(D) 退休工人

解說　**注意標題與粗體字**　難易度 ★★

從標題下面的粗體字 Sponsored by the ... Parent Teacher Association（由……家長教師會主辦）可合理推測，活動的對象是當地的家庭。另外，從詳細內容的 The family-friendly event includes:...（家庭活動包含：……）也可以知道這是為家庭舉辦的活動，因此正確答案是 (B) Local families。

---

2. 關於慈善活動的敘述，何者為非？
(A) 將於下午舉辦。
(B) 將有音樂表演。
(C) 幼齡兒童免費。
(D) 活動包含抽獎。

解說　**注意數字；NOT 問句通常可用消去法解題**　難易度 ★★

從 Tickets（票價）可知，兒童票價為 15 美元，並非免費，因此正確答案是 (C) It is free for young children.。從 Time（時間）可知活動於下午舉行，從 Description（詳細說明）可知有音樂表演，而青少年和兒童的票價則包含抽獎活動，分別與選項 (A)、(B)、(D) 相符，所以都不是正確答案。

---

3. 哪一個計畫將受惠於這次活動？
(A) 舞蹈劇院
(B) 年長者協會
(C) 新學校建設
(D) 音樂與藝術計畫

解說　**注意最後一句**　難易度 ★★

從通知最後一行的粗體字 All Proceeds Go to Our Elementary School "Music and Arts" Project（所有收入將捐給我們國小的「音樂與藝術」計畫）可知，收益將捐給音樂與藝術計畫，因此正確答案是 (D) A music and arts program。

換句話說　正文 Project ➡ 選項 program

1 分鐘 CHECK!

複習「通知、公告、企業內部公告」的閱讀重點及 Day 5 的必背字彙。

「通知、公告、企業內部公告」的閱讀重點

- ☐ 通知、公告、企業內部公告是對多數人宣布、發表特定事項的文章。常考的是關於公共設施規則的變更、活動通知、人事異動或公司內部規則變更、設施改裝等的公司內部公告。

- ☐ 可從標題與粗體字掌握「目的」、「對象」。

- ☐ 規則的細節以條列方式書寫。

- ☐ 最後會在 Note 等處提到洽詢方式或注意事項。

「通知、公告、企業內部公告」的必背字彙

- ☐ change in... 在…的變更
- ☐ Please carefully note... 請小心注意……
- ☐ Remember to... 請記得……
- ☐ be subject to... 受…的約束
- ☐ Please be advised that... 請注意……
- ☐ effective date 生效日
- ☐ remain the same 維持不變
- ☐ be suspended 暫時停止
- ☐ continue to... 繼續…
- ☐ We would like to bring your attention to... 我們想請你注意……
- ☐ penalty fee 罰款
- ☐ description 名 說明，詳細內容

Day6

本日主題

● 徵才相關文章

Day 6 徵才相關文章

徵才相關的文章多半以報紙、網路徵才廣告的形式出題，也是多篇文章測驗常見的題型。另外也會考推薦信、雇用契約等。閱讀徵才廣告時，必須注意「徵才的職務種類」、「徵才原因」、「資格條件」與「待遇」。

● 接待員的徵才廣告

> **Point 1** 前半段寫有公司名稱、徵才的職務種類、徵才原因！

Help Wanted

Carson City Apartment Rentals is seeking a receptionist to staff its new branch office in the West River Mall.

學歷

Education: high school diploma a must, associate's or bachelor's degree preferred

> **Point 2** 資格條件一定會考！

資格條件

Requirements: • Able to interact with the public

• Keyboarding skills　• Punctual　• Flexible

職務內容

Responsibilities: • Message taking　• E-mail writing

• Appointment scheduling　• Basic record-keeping

Working hours: 9:00 - 5:00 Monday-Friday 工作時間
Starting day: August 1st 開始工作日
Salary: Negotiable 薪資
Application Deadline: July 20th 應徵截止日

For details, contact:
To apply for this receptionist opening, please send your résumé with a cover letter to:
Jim Stearns, Manager
Carson City Apartment Rentals
138 Main Street Carson City
Tel. 555-3197

> **Point 3** 應徵所需資料與應徵方式寫在最後！

Point 1 從標題或前半段內容找出公司名稱、徵才的職務種類、徵才原因！

標題或正文開頭部分通常會有「公司名稱」、「徵才的職務種類」、「徵才原因」，請特別注意。

Point 2 資格條件一定會考！

徵才相關的文章中，與資格條件有關的題目很常出現，例如必須具備什麼證照或經驗等。

- 資格條件：requirements/qualifications
- 必要條件：出現 must/essential/required/necessary/needed 的句子
- 加分條件：出現 preferred/preferable/desired/desirable/helpful/ is a plus 的句子
- 職務內容：出現 responsibilities/duties include... / be responsible for... 的句子

Point 3 應徵所需資料、應徵方式與聯絡方式寫在最後！

後半段會有與應徵方法有關的資訊。徵才廣告經常會要求應徵者提出 application（應徵表格）、résumé（履歷表）、recommendation letter/ reference（推薦信），並附上 cover/application letter（求職信）。應徵方式則有 post（郵寄）、e-mail as an attachment（以附加檔案方式用電子郵件傳送）等。

中譯 　　　　　　　　　　　徵人啟事

卡爾森市公寓租賃公司正在尋找一名接待員，進駐西河商場的新分店。

學歷：需有高中學歷，副學士或學士學位更佳
資格條件：可與人群互動‧打字技巧‧守時‧靈活
職務內容：記錄訊息‧撰寫電子郵件‧安排行程‧基本記錄工作
工作時間：週一至週五9點至5點
開始工作日：8月1日
薪資：面議
應徵截止日：7月20日

欲知詳情，請聯絡：
想應徵此接待員職缺，請將履歷表和求職信寄至：
經理　吉姆‧斯特恩斯
卡爾森市公寓租賃公司
卡爾森市緬因街 138 號
電話：555-3197

---

1 與資格條件有關的題目
注意 Requirements（資格條件）或 Qualifications（資格）項目中提到的條件。

題目

- What is a requirement for the job?（應徵這份工作的資格條件是什麼？）
- What is NOT a requirement for the job?（哪一項不是應徵這份工作的資格條件？）
- What is NOT required for job applicants?（哪一項不是應徵者必備的資格條件？）

文中的表達方式

- At least 5 years of experience in similar positions is essential.
  （需有至少五年的相關工作經驗。）
- French language skills (a plus)（法語能力〔加分條件〕）

2 與職務內容有關的題目
注意 Responsibilities（職務內容）項目中提到的工作內容，或者是出現 responsibilities/duties include...（職務內容包含…）或 be responsible for...（負責…）的句子。

題目

- According to the want ad, what is NOT included in the job responsibilities?
  （根據徵人廣告的內容，哪一項不包含在工作內容裡？）

文中的表達方式

- The assistant director of the personnel department will be responsible for assisting the director in supervising staff, including employee training and promotion.
  （人事部助理主任將負責協助主任管理員工，包含員工訓練及晉升等事務。）

3 與應徵所需資料、應徵方式、應徵截止日有關的題目
這些資訊大多寫在最後。

題目

- What should the candidate submit with an application?
  （應徵者應提出應徵表格和什麼資料？）
- How should an applicant respond to this ad?
  （應徵者應如何回覆這則廣告？）

- When is the deadline to apply for the position?
  （此職缺的應徵截止日是什麼時候？）

- Please mail/post a résumé with two recommendations and a cover letter to:
  ... on or before Friday May 5.
  （請將履歷表、兩封推薦信及求職信，最遲於 5 月 5 日星期五寄至……）
- Download the application from our Web site (www.rm&m.com) and e-mail as
  an attached file to: HRrm&m@widenet.com by March 21.
  （從我們的網站 (www.rm&m.com) 下載應徵表格，並於 3 月 21 日前將表格以附加檔案
  方式用電子郵件寄至：HRrm&m@widenet.com。）
- Interested candidates should submit their applications stating their experience
  as well as current and expected compensation by e-mail no later than June 8.
  （有意應徵者應在應徵表格內說明自己的經歷、目前待遇以及期望薪資，最遲於 6 月 8
  日將應徵表格以電子郵件寄出。）

DAY
6

徵才相關文章

加分表現

在西方社會，應徵工作時通常需要前上司提出推薦信 (recommendation
letter = reference)，請記住這種時候常用的句型。

- This is a recommendation letter for Mary Chung, who is applying to your
  firm for the position of public relations director.
  （這是為鍾瑪麗所寫的推薦信，用以應徵貴公司公共關係主任一職。）

Questions 1-3 refer to the following advertisement.

SHALOMAR CORPORATION

A great opportunity awaits you to become a member of the management team of a chain of luxury hotels that is based in Malaysia. Our head office is in Kuala Lumpur. We are now opening new branches in Singapore and Indonesia.

We are seeking

Position: Director of Sales and Marketing
Sector: Hotel and Resort Management

Qualifications

- Malaysian nationality (essential)
- Bachelor's degree or higher (required)
- Experience in hotel business for minimum of 5 years (necessary)
- Fluency in Malay and English (needed)
- Chinese language skills (a plus)
- Willingness to relocate to new locations abroad (a must)

We offer attractive remuneration and benefits along with excellent working conditions.

Please mail an application letter with résumé and two recommendations to:

Director of Personnel
Shalomar Corporation
75/104 Ocean Tower
Randolph Plaza
Kuala Lumpur

1. Why is there most likely a vacant position for director of sales and marketing?

   (A) The company is expanding its operations.
   (B) The current director has resigned.
   (C) The hotel needs to increase occupancy rates.
   (D) The corporation is starting a resort division.

2. What is NOT required for job applicants?

   (A) Willingness to work overseas
   (B) A university degree
   (C) Fluency in Chinese
   (D) Malaysian citizenship

3. How should an applicant respond to this ad?

   (A) By e-mailing an inquiry
   (B) By applying online
   (C) By posting an application
   (D) By telephoning the director of personnel

徵才相關文章

中譯 問題 1-3：請看以下廣告。

夏洛瑪公司

想成為馬來西亞奢華連鎖飯店管理團隊的一員嗎？大好機會正在等著你。我們的總公司位於吉隆坡，[1]現在正計畫於新加坡及印尼開設分公司。

我們正在尋找
職位：業務行銷主任
部門：飯店及渡假村管理

資格條件
● 馬來西亞國籍（必要條件）
● 學士學位或以上（必要條件）
● 至少五年飯店業經驗（必要條件）
● 馬來語及英語流利（必要條件）
● [2]中文能力（加分條件）
● 願意派駐海外新店點（必要條件）

我們提供誘人的薪酬與福利，以及絕佳的工作條件。

[3]請將求職信、履歷表及兩封推薦信寄至：

人事主任
夏洛瑪公司
吉隆坡藍道夫廣場
海洋塔 75/104 號

單字

□ await 動 等待
□ chain 名 連鎖店
□ luxury 名 奢華
□ head office 總公司
□ branch 名 分公司，分店
□ sector 名 部門
□ bachelor's degree 學士學位

□ minimum 名 最小量，最低限度
□ fluency 名 流利
□ willingness 名 樂意
□ relocate 動 調動
□ remuneration 名 薪水，酬勞
□ benefit 名 津貼，福利

1. 產生業務行銷主任一職缺最有可能的原因是什麼？
   (A) 公司正在擴大營業。
   (B) 現任主任辭職了。
   (C) 飯店需要增加入住率。
   (D) 公司正要開設渡假村部門。

解說 從廣告前半段找出徵才原因
難易度 ★★

從第三句 We are now opening new branches in Singapore and Indonesia.（現在正計畫於新加坡及印尼開設分公司。）可知，該公司正在擴大營業，可能因此需要徵才。正確答案是 (A) The company is expanding its operations.。

換句話說 正文 opening new branches ➡ 選項 expanding its operations

2. 哪一項不是應徵者必備的資格條件？
   (A) 願意到海外工作
   (B) 大學學歷
   (C) 中文流利
   (D) 為馬來西亞公民

解說 找出 Qualifications
難易度 ★★

從 Qualifications（資格條件）的第五點 Chinese language skills (a plus)（中文能力〔加分條件〕）可知，懂中文是加分條件，非必要條件，因此正確答案是 (C) Fluency in Chinese。

3. 應徵者應如何回覆這則廣告？
   (A) 寄電子郵件詢問細節
   (B) 線上申請
   (C) 郵寄應徵表格
   (D) 打電話給人事主任

解說 應徵方式要看廣告最後
難易度 ★★★

從廣告最後的 Please mail an application letter with résumé and two recommendations to:...（請將求職信、履歷表及兩封推薦信寄至：……）可知，應徵者必須郵寄特定的應徵資料，因此正確答案是 (C) By posting an application。注意 mail 是「郵寄」的意思。

換句話說 正文 mail ➡ 選項 posting

DAY 6

徵才相關文章

Questions **1-4** refer to the following advertisement.

Ralston Mining and Manufacturing
Northern Territories
Australia
www.rm&m.com

Ralston Mining and Manufacturing is inviting applicants for the position of

ASSISTANT ACCOUNTING MANAGER

The assistant accounting manager is responsible for helping the accounting manager to oversee all bookkeeping and budgeting. The job involves reviewing and reporting earnings, expenditures, and company transactions.

Qualifications of the successful candidate:
- B.A. or B.S. in accounting required
- at least 5 years of experience in similar positions essential
- a CPA (certified public accountant) certification desirable
- ability to communicate well in spoken and written English required
- high-level proficiency in accounting and spreadsheet software applications necessary (knowledge of ERP system is desirable)

Initial salary will be commensurate with the successful applicant's qualifications and previous experience. Interested candidates should submit their applications electronically by e-mail, stating in full their qualifications and experience, as well as current and expected compensation.

Download the application from our Web site (*www.rm&m.com*) and e-mail as an attached file to: *HRrm&m@widenet.com*

1. In what professional area is the position?

    (A) Personnel recruitment
    (B) Financial record-keeping
    (C) Strategic planning
    (D) Research and development

2. What is NOT stated in the job responsibilities?

    (A) Administering budgets
    (B) Managing staff
    (C) Making earning reports
    (D) Tracking expenses

3. What is NOT stated as a qualification requirement?

    (A) A degree in accounting
    (B) A CPA certification
    (C) Professional experience
    (D) Computer literacy

4. What should the candidate submit with an application?

    (A) Salary expectations
    (B) Letters of recommendation
    (C) A list of references
    (D) Professional certifications

中譯 問題 1-4：請看以下廣告。

萊爾斯頓礦業製造公司
澳洲北領地
www.rm&m.com

萊爾斯頓礦業製造公司[1] 正在邀請求職者應徵

會計副理一職

會計副理要負責協助會計經理[2] 監管所有簿記及預算。工作內容包含檢查與報告收入、支出及公司交易。

成功應徵者的資格條件：
- 需有會計文學士或理學士學位
- 需有至少五年的相關工作經驗
- [3] 具合格會計師資格者佳
- 需具備良好英文說寫能力
- 需精通會計及試算表軟體應用程式（了解 ERP 系統更佳）

起薪將依應徵者的資格條件及過去經歷而定。有意應徵者應以電子郵件寄出應徵表格，並[4] 在表格內完整說明自己的資格條件、經歷、目前待遇以及期望薪資。

從我們的網站 (www.rm&m.com) 下載應徵表格，並將表格以附加檔案方式用電子郵件寄至：HRrm&m@widenet.com。

單字

- □ oversee 動 管理，監督
- □ bookkeeping 名 簿記
- □ budgeting 名 編列預算
- □ earnings 名 收入
- □ expenditure 名 支出
- □ transaction 名 交易
- □ candidate 名 應徵者
- □ B.A. 文學士（即 Bachelor of Arts）
- □ B.S. 理學士（即 Bachelor of Science）
- □ certified 形 合格的，經證明的
- □ proficiency 名 精通
- □ initial salary 起薪
- □ be commensurate with... 與…相稱的
- □ submit 動 提出
- □ electronically 副 以電子方式
- □ compensation 名 酬勞，薪水

1. 這個職位屬於哪一個專業領域？
- (A) 人事招募
- (B) 金融簿記
- (C) 策略計畫
- (D) 研究發展

解說　從廣告前半段找出徵才的職務種類

難易度　★★

從第一段的 is inviting applicants for the position of ASSISTANT ACCOUNTING MANAGER（正在邀請求職者應徵會計副理一職）可知，該職位是屬於金融簿記方面的工作，因此正確答案是 (B) Financial record-keeping。事先記住部門、職務相關的單字吧。

換句話說　正文 ACCOUNTING ➡ 選項 financial

---

2. 哪一項不包含在工作內容裡？
- (A) 管理預算
- (B) 管理員工
- (C) 製作營收報告
- (D) 追蹤支出

解說　找出有 be responsible for... 與 involve... 的句子

難易度　★

從 is responsible for 後面的內容可知，工作內容為 oversee all bookkeeping and budgeting（監管所有簿記及預算）；The job involves 後面則提到 reviewing and reporting earnings, expenditures（檢查與報告收入、支出），分別與 (A)、(C)、(D) 相符。沒有提到的是 (B) Managing staff。

---

3. 哪一項不是應徵這份工作的必要條件？
- (A) 會計學位
- (B) 合格會計師資格
- (C) 專業經歷
- (D) 電腦能力

解說　找出 Qualifications

難易度　★★

從 Qualifications（資格條件）的第三點 a CPA certification desirable（具合格會計師資格者佳）可知，有合格會計師資格只是加分條件，非必要條件，因此正確答案是 (B) A CPA certification。

---

4. 應徵者在應徵表格中要提出什麼？
- (A) 期望薪資
- (B) 推薦信
- (C) 推薦人名單
- (D) 專業證書

解說　應徵資料要看廣告最後

難易度　★★

從廣告後半段的 Interested candidates should submit（有意應徵者應寄出）後面的內容可知，應徵者必須說明其 qualifications and experience（資格條件、經歷）以及 current and expected compensation（目前待遇以及期望薪資），因此正確答案是 (A) Salary expectations。

換句話說　正文 expected compensation ➡ 選項 Salary expectations

Questions 1-3 refer to the following contract.

Employment Contract

Employer: Fashion Apparel International
Position: Sales Associate
Main Place of Employment: 6th Street Store

Duties: To stock and to arrange garment displays and to assist customers in purchases.

Conditions: Your normal working hours are 20 hours per week at the following times: Saturdays and Sundays 12:00 P.M. to 9:00 P.M. and one evening a week from 5:00 P.M. to 9:00 P.M. You will have a meal break of 1 hour per day on Saturdays and Sundays which is not working time and which is not paid.

Remuneration: Your salary will be paid at the following rate: £9 per hour. Your salary will be paid on the last day of each month by bank transfer.

Place of employment: Your normal place of work will be the 6th Street store, but you may occasionally be required to work from time to time at other locations within the downtown area.

Commencement of employment: To be determined

Name of employee: Leah White

I agree to the foregoing terms and conditions: *Leah White, March 12*

---

1. What kind of company is Fashion Apparel International?

    (A) A manufacturer
    (B) A retail store
    (C) A wholesale distributor
    (D) A design company

2. How many days will Ms. White probably work each week?

    (A) One
    (B) Two
    (C) Three
    (D) Four

3. All of the following employment conditions for the position have been decided EXCEPT

    (A) Hourly pay
    (B) Employment duties
    (C) Starting date
    (D) Lunch break

徵才相關文章

中譯 問題 1-3：請看以下契約。

雇用契約

雇主：國際時尚服裝公司
職位：[1]銷售人員
主要工作地點：第六街分店

工作內容：進貨，安排服裝陳列，[1]協助顧客購物。

工作條件：正常工作時間為每週 20 小時，時間如下：[2]週六及週日中午 12 點至晚上 9 點，另外每週有一天為傍晚 5 點至晚上 9 點。週六及週日兩天各有一小時的用餐時間，不列入工時亦不給薪。

薪資：薪資為時薪九英鎊，薪水將於每個月最後一天以銀行轉帳方式支付。

工作地點：平常工作地點為第六街分店，但有時候可能需要到市中心其他分店工作。

[3]工作開始日：尚待決定

員工姓名：莉亞‧懷特

我同意以上條款和條件：*莉亞‧懷特，3月12日*

單字

□ employment 名 雇用
□ apparel 名 服裝
□ sales associate 銷售人員
□ stock 動 進貨
□ garment 名 服裝，衣著
□ display 名 陳列，展示

□ occasionally 副 偶爾
□ commencement 名 開始
□ determine 動 決定
□ foregoing 形 前述的
□ terms and conditions 條款和條件

1. (B)　**2.** (C)　**3.** (C)

1. 國際時尚服裝是哪一種公司？
(A) 製造商
(B) 零售店
(C) 批發商
(D) 設計公司

解說 **從職務種類與工作內容判斷產業類別**

難易度 ★★

從 Position（職位）可知，該公司徵求的是 Sales Associate（銷售人員）。另外從 Duties（工作內容）可知，工作內容包含 assist customers in purchases（協助顧客購物），也就是零售店銷售人員的工作，因此正確答案是 (B) A retail store。

2. 懷特小姐每週可能要工作幾天？
(A) 一天
(B) 二天
(C) 三天
(D) 四天

解說 **找出 Conditions**

難易度 ★

從 Conditions（工作條件）中的 Saturdays and Sundays 12:00 P.M. to 9:00 P.M. and one evening a week, from 5:00 P.M. to 9:00 P.M.（週六及週日中午 12 點至晚上 9 點，另外每週有一天為傍晚 5 點至晚上 9 點。）可知，工作時間是週六、日及一個平日晚上，共三天，因此正確答案是 (C) Three。

3. 除了以下哪一項之外，關於這個職位的工作條件都已經確定了？
(A) 時薪
(B) 工作內容
(C) 開始日
(D) 午餐休息時間

解說 **看清楚契約內容**

難易度 ★★

Commencement of employment（工作開始日）寫著 To be determined（尚待決定），也就是說開始上班日尚未確定，因此正確答案是 (C) Starting date。記住 to be determined 這個說法。Remuneration（薪資）提到薪水，Duties（工作內容）則寫出工作內容，Conditions（工作條件）最後則寫了用餐休息時間，分別與選項 (A)、(B)、(D) 相符，因此非正確答案。

換句話說　正文 Commencement of employment ➡ 選項 Starting date

1 分鐘 CHECK!

複習「徵才相關文章」的閱讀重點及 Day 6 的必背字彙。

「徵才相關文章」的閱讀重點

☐ 經常出現在測驗裡的是徵才廣告。此外，推薦信、雇用契約等也很常考。

☐ 徵才廣告可在標題或前半段找到公司名稱、徵才的職務種類、徵才原因。

☐ 記住應徵的資格條件分為必要條件和非必要（加分）條件。
必要條件關鍵字：must/essential/required/necessary/needed
非必要（加分）條件關鍵字：preferred/preferable/desired/desirable/
helpful/ is a plus

☐ 應徵所需資料、應徵方式、聯絡方式寫在後半段。

「徵才相關文章」的必背字彙

☐ branch 名 分公司，分店
☐ bachelor's degree 學士學位
☐ qualification 名 資格，能力
☐ responsibility 名 職務內容
☐ starting day 工作開始日
☐ salary 名 薪水
☐ earnings 名 收入
☐ application/cover letter 求職信
☐ deadline 名 應徵截止日

☐ apply for... 應徵…（職缺）
☐ résumé 名 履歷表
☐ be responsible for... 負責…
☐ position 名 職位，職務
☐ compensation 名 酬勞，薪水
☐ head office 總公司
☐ fluency 名 流利
☐ benefit 名 津貼，福利
☐ working conditions 工作條件

Day 7

本日主題
● 新聞報導

Day 7 新聞報導

出現在閱讀測驗中的新聞報導，大多與企業（新公司成立、合併、倒閉、收購）、得獎消息公布、事故有關。相較於其他類型的文章，新聞報導使用的單字較難，不過只要掌握重點，就能夠提高閱讀效率。

閱讀商業、企業相關的報導時，必須注意商業用語。

STEP 1　看看這類文章的閱讀重點！

● 擴大事業經營的報導

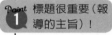

CoffeeTime Expands in China

CoffeeTime, the largest coffee chain in the world, announced yesterday that it planned to increase its capital investment in China by 25 percent next year by renovating stores and offering free wireless Internet services to attract customers.

CoffeeTime also announced that it plans to open 150 to 175 additional restaurants in China, adding to its more than 1,000 already operating in the country, Richard Chang, head of its China operations, said yesterday. That will lead to the creation of 10,000 new jobs, according to Mr. Chang.

CoffeeTime is also launching an advertising campaign with the motto, "It's time to relax," to mark the 20th anniversary of opening its first restaurant in China.

Point 1 從標題與開頭部分掌握主旨！

報導的主旨寫在標題或開頭部分。注意新聞報導慣用的表達方式，快速掌握主旨。

Point 2 掌握新聞報導的架構！

新聞報導的鋪陳有一定的架構。事業擴大、收購合併、得獎消息公布、事故等新聞報導經常出現在測驗中，請務必掌握這類報導的架構。。
- 事業擴大、收購合併的報導架構：大多是說明經過，最後歸納出今後的方針、預測的結果。
- 得獎消息公布的報導架構：大多是說明獎項名稱、得獎者過去的成績。
- 事故的報導架構：大多是依照「事故發生的地點與時間、原因、經過、結果」的順序說明。

Point 3 注意新聞報導中的人名、職稱、組織名稱！

題目通常會問，在眾多人物當中「○○是誰？」，問該人物的職稱、經歷、隸屬的組織名稱等。

Point 4 注意內含慣用說法的關鍵句！

新聞報導經常出現 announced/reported that...（發表了／報告了…），這是提及報導主旨的句子，因此閱讀時要注意內含 announced/reported that... 的關鍵句。

中譯   咖啡時光在中國擴大營業

世界最大的連鎖咖啡店咖啡時光昨天宣布，明年將整修旗下店面，並提供免費的無線網路，以吸引消費者上門，他們計畫在中國增加 25% 的投資。

中國營運主管張理查昨天表示，咖啡時光也宣布計畫於中國再開設 150 至 175 家分店，加入該國已經營業的一千多家分店的行列。根據張的說法，這將創造出一萬個新的工作機會。

咖啡時光也開始進行一波以「是時候放鬆了」為標語的廣告活動，慶祝在中國第一家分店開幕 20 週年。

---

1 與報導的目的或主旨有關的題目
報導的目的或主旨大多寫在標題，如果沒有標題，通常可以從內含慣用說法的關鍵句推測出正確答案。

題目

- What is the main purpose of the article?（這篇文章的主要目的為何？）
- What is the article mainly about?（這篇文章主要在說什麼？）

【標題】

- 標題 American Automobiles Names New Vice President
  （美國汽車任命新副總裁）

  ⬇

  答案 To announce the hiring of an executive（宣布雇用高階經理人）

- 標題 Flaming Tours Opens New Office In Miami
  （火紅旅行社於邁阿密開設新辦公室）

  ⬇

  答案 To inform people about the company expansion
  （通知大家有關公司擴張一事）

- 標題 The Regent Hotel to Open Soon（麗晶酒店即將開幕）

  ⬇

  答案 The opening of new accommodations（新的住宿設施開幕）

- 標題 Calgary's City Council selected high school teacher Nancy Smith as its
  "Best Teacher of the Year"
  （卡加利市議會選出高中教師南西‧史密斯為「年度最佳教師」）

  ⬇

  答案 An award announcement（公布得獎消息）

- 標題 WEIGHT-LIFTING IS HEALTHY（舉重有益健康）

  ⬇

  答案 To point out the benefits of weight-lifting（指出舉重的好處）

【內含慣用說法的關鍵句】

如果從報導的標題無法看出目的或主旨，看看正文裡的關鍵句吧。

● 關鍵句 ABC Technology Corporation announced today that it will merge with
　　　　XYZ Corporation.（ABC 科技公司今天宣布將與 XYZ 公司合併。）
　　　　⬇
　答案 A combining of two companies（兩家公司合併）

● 關鍵句 Washington Tires reported today that it plans to build a new factory
　　　　in Saigon.（華盛頓輪胎今天報告，計畫於西貢興建新的工廠。）
　　　　⬇
　答案 To announce the expansion of the company（宣布公司擴張）

2 與職業有關的題目

出現在報導中的人物的職業也很常考。職稱通常寫在人名旁邊。

題目

● Who is A?（A 是誰？）

文中的表達方式

● Mr. Robin Hird, president of the Cosmo Automobile Manufacturing Company,
also commented on the news, saying that...
（科茲摩汽車製造廠的總裁羅賓・赫德先生也對這則新聞發表了評論，他表示……）

加分表現

★ 新聞報導常用字彙

記住報導中經常使用的收購、合併等與公司有關的單字，能夠更快推測出正確答案。

● M&A (= mergers & acquisitions) 併購　　　● acquire 動 購買，收購
● acquisition 名 購買，收購　　　　　　　　● merge 動 合併
● merger 名 合併　　　　　　　　　　　　　● joint venture 合資企業
● incorporate 動 組成公司　　　　　　　　　● stock 名 股份，股票

「倒閉、解雇」的相關單字，也請一併記住。

● go bankrupt 破產　　　　　　　　　　　　● bankruptcy 名 破產
● lay off... 解雇…　　　　　　　　　　　　● dismiss 動 開除

Questions 1-4 refer to the following article.

LOCAL BUSINESS EXECUTIVE NAMED "CONSULTANT OF THE YEAR"

Lakeville's Chamber of Commerce named local business employee Tracy Campbell as its "Consultant of the Year" at its annual awards banquet on Friday. —[1]—. The Chamber is an independent organization supported by businesses in the greater Lakeville area.

Ms. Campbell is the head of educational training for Business Solutions Inc. (BSI). —[2]—. BSI provides business consulting services to small- and mid-sized firms throughout the northwest region, offering seminars and workshops to middle level management. The firm advises supervisors on how to more efficiently use meeting time and conduct office communication. —[3]—.

According to the Chamber, Ms. Campbell's practical training seminars helped companies, on average, reduce e-mail volumes by 20 percent, raise e-mail quality by 30 percent, and improve electronic information management by 35 percent. —[4]—.

---

1. What is this article mainly about?

    (A) An award announcement
    (B) A new business
    (C) A company expansion
    (D) A corporate report

2. Who is Ms. Campbell?

    (A) A company owner
    (B) President of the Chamber of Commerce
    (C) A business consultant
    (D) A local teacher

3. According to the article, what effect do Business Solutions workshops have on a company?

    (A) They improve management decisions.
    (B) They make records more detailed.
    (C) They decrease the number of e-mails.
    (D) They lower staff turnover.

4. In which of the positions marked [1], [2], [3], and [4] does the following sentence best belong?
"It also provides guidance on information security systems."

    (A) [1]
    (B) [2]
    (C) [3]
    (D) [4]

中譯 問題 1-4：請看以下文章。

[1]地方企業的主管獲提名為「年度最佳顧問」

雷克維爾商會於週五的年度頒獎晚宴中，[1]提名當地一企業的員工崔西‧坎貝爾為「年度最佳顧問」。—[1]—。該商會是由大雷克維爾地區商界所支持的一個獨立機構。

[2]坎貝爾小姐是商業決策公司 (BSI) 的教育訓練主管。—[2]—。[2]BSI 對西北區全區的中小型企業提供商業諮詢服務，並為中階管理人員提供講座及工作坊。[4]該公司就如何更有效率運用會議時間、如何進行辦公室溝通等議題，對管理階層提出建議。—[3]—。

據商會表示，坎貝爾小姐的實務訓練講座[3]平均能幫助企業減少 20% 的電子郵件量，提升 30% 的郵件品質，並改善 35% 的電子資訊管理。—[4]—。

單字

□ name 動 提名
□ consultant 名 顧問
□ chamber of commerce 商會
□ awards banquet 頒獎晚宴
□ management 名 管理階層

□ supervisor 名 管理人員
□ efficiently 副 有效率地
□ conduct 動 實施，進行
□ volume 名 量

1. (A)　　**2.** (C)　　**3.** (C)　　**4.** (C)

1. 這篇文章主要在說什麼？
(A) 獎項宣布
(B) 新公司
(C) 公司擴張
(D) 公司報告

從標題或開頭部分找出報導的主旨

難易度 ★

從標題與開頭部分的 named local business employee Tracy Campbell as its "Consultant of the Year"（提名當地一企業的員工崔西‧坎貝爾為「年度最佳顧問」）可知，這是公布得獎消息的報導，正確答案是 (A) An award announcement。

2. 誰是坎貝爾小姐？
(A) 公司所有人
(B) 商會會長
(C) 商業顧問
(D) 地方教師

注意人名與職稱

難易度 ★

第二段的 Ms. Campbell is the head of educational training for BSI.（坎貝爾小姐是商業決策公司的教育訓練主管。）寫出坎貝爾小姐的職稱，接著指出 BSI provides business consulting services...（BSI 提供商業諮詢服務……），也就是說，坎貝爾小姐是商業顧問公司的教育訓練主管，所以正確答案是 (C) A business consultant。

3. 根據文章內容，商業決策公司的工作坊對企業有什麼影響？
(A) 它們能改善管理決策。
(B) 它們能更詳細記錄資料。
(C) 它們能減少電子郵件的數量。
(D) 它們能降低員工的流動率。

注意最後一句

難易度 ★

從第三段的 helped companies, on average, reduce e-mail volumes by 20 percent（平均能幫助企業減少 20% 的電子郵件量）可知，工作坊能幫助公司減少郵件數量，因此正確答案是 (C) They decrease the number of e-mails。

正文 reduce e-mail volumes ➡ 選項 decrease the number of e-mails

4. 下列句子最適合放在 [1]、[2]、[3]、[4] 哪一個位置？
「它也提供資訊安全系統的指導。」
(A) [1]
(B) [2]
(C) [3]
(D) [4]

注意插入句的副詞

難易度 ★★

插入句的內容與 BSI 公司提供的服務有關，從句中的副詞 also（也）可知，插入句前面提到了該公司的服務。第二段最後一句 The firm advises supervisors...（該公司對管理階層提出建議……）提及該公司的服務，插入句放在這句話後面非常適合，因此正確答案是 (C) [3]。

DAY 7

新聞報導

Questions 1-4 refer to the following article.

1st National and Merchants Banks to Merge

The CEO of 1st National Bank and the president of Merchants Bank officially announced this morning that their two financial firms have agreed to merge. The agreement followed an unsuccessful effort by Merchants Bank in January to acquire 1st National in a stock buyout. The shareholders of 1st National's stock rejected the offer as too low.

In February, executives of the two banks entered negotiations to combine their operations, and in March, the boards of directors of both banks tentatively approved the merger, with the details to be worked out and approved in April. Yesterday, the agreement was concluded on schedule.

The new bank will be called 1st National and Merchants Bank. The firm will combine 1st National Bank's existing banking system, situated largely in urban areas, with Merchants' extensive network of rural and small-town branches. The joint capitalization of the banks will make 1st National and Merchants the third largest bank in the nation. Each bank is expected to trim 10 percent of its workforce.

1. What does this article announce?

    (A) A corporate bankruptcy

    (B) A combining of two companies

    (C) A buyout proposal

    (D) A new company spin off

2. When was the merger proposal first discussed?

    (A) January

    (B) February

    (C) March

    (D) April

3. According to the article, where are most of 1st National Bank's offices located?

    (A) In foreign capitals

    (B) In large cities

    (C) In medium-sized towns

    (D) In rural areas

4. According to the article, which of the following is true?

    (A) The new bank will be called "1st National."

    (B) Merchants Bank has offices only in urban areas.

    (C) The new bank will increase its workforce.

    (D) Both banks may lay off some of their employees.

中譯 問題 1-4：請看以下文章。

¹第一國際銀行和商業銀行合併

第一國際銀行的執行長和商業銀行總經理今天早上正式宣布，兩家金融機構同意合併。在此之前，商業銀行曾於一月試圖以收購股份的方式買下第一國際銀行，但以失敗告終。第一國際銀行的股東以出價過低為由拒絕其收購。

²二月，兩家銀行的高層人員進入公司合併的協商；三月，兩家銀行的董事會暫時同意合併案，接著於四月擬出細節並通過。昨日，已按原訂計畫完成協議。

新銀行的名稱將會是第一國際商業銀行，公司將結合³第一國際銀行大部分位於都會區的現有銀行體系，以及商業銀行於郊區及小城鎮分行的密集網絡。兩銀行的聯合資本將使第一國際商業銀行成為國內第三大銀行。⁴兩家銀行預計將各裁減 10% 的人力。

單字

- □ CEO 名 執行長
  （即 chief executive officer）
- □ president 名 總經理
- □ officially 副 正式地
- □ financial firm 金融機構
- □ buyout 名 收購
- □ shareholder 名 股東
- □ negotiation 名 協商
- □ board of directors 董事會
- □ tentatively 副 暫時地

- □ approve 動 同意；認可
- □ situate 動 使位於
- □ urban 形 城市的，都會的
- □ extensive 形 廣大的
- □ rural 形 地方的，鄉下的
- □ joint 形 聯合的，共有的
- □ capitalization 名 資本額
- □ trim 動 削減
- □ workforce 名 勞動力，人力

1. 這篇文章宣布了什麼？
(A) 公司破產
(B) 兩家公司合併
(C) 收購計畫
(D) 新公司分拆

解說 從標題或開頭部分找出報導的主旨

(難易度) ★

從報導的標題 1st National and Merchants Banks to Merge（第一國際銀行和商業銀行合併）可知，這是公布公司合併消息的報導，因此正確答案是 (B) A combining of two companies。

換句話說 正文 1st National and Merchants Banks to Merge
➡ 選項 combining of two companies

---

2. 合併提案第一次討論是什麼時候？
(A) 一月
(B) 二月
(C) 三月
(D) 四月

解說 找出月分

(難易度) ★★★

從第二段的 In February, executives of the two banks entered negotiations to combine their operations...（二月，兩家銀行的高層人員進入公司合併的協商……）可知，二月開始協商，也就是第一次討論合併案，因此正確答案是 (B) February。

---

3. 根據文章內容，第一國際銀行的辦公室大多位於何處？
(A) 在其他國家的首都
(B) 在大城市
(C) 在中型城鎮
(D) 在郊區

解說 找出 1st National Bank

(難易度) ★★

從第三段的 1st National Bank's existing banking system, situated largely in urban areas（第一國際銀行大部分位於都會區的現有銀行體系）可知，第一國際銀行大多位於都市，因此正確答案是 (B) In large cities。

換句話說 正文 urban areas ➡ 選項 large cities

---

4. 根據文章內容，以下何者為真？
(A) 新銀行將稱為「第一國際」。
(B) 商業銀行只在都會區有辦公室。
(C) 新銀行將增加人力。
(D) 兩家銀行可能都會裁減部分員工。

解說 注意文章最後一句和預測的結果

(難易度) ★★★

從報導最後一句 Each bank is expected to trim 10 percent of its workforce.（兩家銀行預計將各裁減 10% 的人力。）可知，兩家銀行將裁減人力，因此正確答案是 (D) Both banks may lay off some of their employees.。像這類與併購有關的報導，注意數字部分通常就能夠導出正確答案。

換句話說 正文 trim ➡ 選項 lay off
正文 workforce ➡ 選項 employees

DAY 7

新聞報導

Questions 1-4 refer to the following article.

Service Halted Two Hours on Central Subway

Transit officials announced that all train service on the central subway line was suspended yesterday due to human error.

Apparently, construction workers working on the city water system mistakenly shut off the power supply to a portion of the subway system between 3rd Street and Market Avenue downtown. This resulted in a halt to the operation of all trains on the central line from 1:10 P.M. to 3:12 P.M. —[1]—.

As a result, passengers on the subway were delayed. —[2]—. Mark Javis, a local business executive who was returning from lunch when the trains were halted, complained when interviewed by a reporter, "I missed two important meetings in the afternoon as a result of the shutdown." —[3]—.

According to Ralph Jacobsen, chief city engineer, trains returned to normal service as soon as the cause of the blackout was identified. Transit officials reported that no passengers were injured. —[4]—. They apologized for the delays, but also observed that because the suspension did not occur during rush hour, the number of passengers who were inconvenienced was limited.

1. How long were the trains stopped?

(A) For one hour
(B) For two hours
(C) For three hours
(D) For four hours

2. Why was train service temporarily suspended?

(A) There was a train accident that caused injuries.
(B) A new electric train was being tested.
(C) An electrical system was mistakenly turned off.
(D) There was a flood in the subway.

3. Who is Mr. Jacobsen?

(A) A business executive
(B) A technician
(C) A construction worker
(D) A reporter

4. In which of the positions marked [1], [2], [3], and [4] does the following sentence best belong?
"Several other passengers en route to the airport said they missed their flights."

(A) [1]
(B) [2]
(C) [3]
(D) [4]

中譯　問題 1-4：請看以下文章。

[1]地鐵中央線暫停服務兩小時

運輸局官員宣布，昨天地鐵中央線所有電車服務[2]因人為因素而暫停。

顯然地，都市自來水系統的[2]建築工人誤關了市中心第三街和市場大道之間部分地下鐵系統的電力，導致中央線所有電車自下午 1 點 10 分至 3 點 12 分暫時停駛。—[1]—。

搭乘地鐵的乘客因此受到延誤。—[2]—。當地一位企業主管[4]馬克‧賈維斯在電車停擺時正用完午餐要回辦公室，他接受記者採訪時抱怨道：「因為停駛的關係，我錯過下午兩場重要的會議。」—[3]—。

據[3]都市總工程師勞夫‧傑考伯森表示，停電原因一經確認後，電車立即恢復正常營運。運輸局官員表示沒有乘客受傷。—[4]—。他們為延遲一事道歉，但也表示，由於停駛不是發生在尖峰時段，因此感到不便的乘客人數有限。

單字

□ halt 動 停止
□ mistakenly 副 錯誤地
□ shut off... 關掉…
□ power supply 電源
□ portion 名 部分

□ shutdown 名 停擺
□ blackout 名 停電
□ identify 動 確認
□ observe 動 說，評論
□ inconvenience 動 給…造成不便

Day8

本日主題

● 說明書、契約、保證書

Day 8 | 說明書、契約、保證書

在說明書、契約、保證書這一類文章中，常出現在測驗中的是電子產品操作說明書、服務維修契約、保證書。先習慣這類文章的閱讀重點與關鍵字吧。若是使用說明書，閱讀的同時必須確認條列項目中的「正確使用方式」、「使用步驟」，以及後半段的「注意事項」。

STEP 1　看看這類文章的閱讀重點！

● 冰箱的使用說明書　 注意標題！

YOUR NEW REFRIGERATOR: USE AND CARE GUIDE

After you unpack your new refrigerator, please follow these directions:

- Plug the power cord into an electrical socket: 正確的使用方式！
  - Set the refrigerator control on 4.
  - Allow 24 hours for the refrigerator and freezer temperatures to stabilize before adjusting the temperature again.

- If the refrigerator is too warm or too cold, use the + or - settings to raise or lower the temperature in the freezer or refrigerator compartment. The temperature control range for both compartments is 1 (warmest) through 7 (coldest).

- Please Note: Changing either control will have some effect on the temperature of the other compartment. 注意事項

- The Door Alarm will alert you when one of the doors has been left open for five minutes. When this happens, an alarm will sound every few seconds until the door is closed. 留意注意事項及有 not 的句子！

保固失效之例

Any damage as a result of improper installation is NOT covered by warranty. If you are unsure of how to correctly install your new refrigerator, call customer service to receive technical support.

Call the toll-free number at 1-800-555-5687 to speak to our trained customer service technicians.

Point 1 閱讀時注意標題與格式！

從標題判斷這是什麼產品的 instructions / use and care guide（使用說明書）、contract（契約）或 warranty（保證書），並找出產品名稱。不論是使用說明書、契約或保證書，往往會有固定的資訊。

● 使用說明書的資訊依以下順序列出：產品名稱、使用步驟、注意事項（在什麼情況下保固將失效等事項）、聯絡方式。

● 契約的資訊依以下順序列出：設備名稱 (Equipment's Name)、簽約日 (Contract Date)、契約期間 (Contract Term)、契約內容 (Contract Conditions)、服務條款 (Conditions of Service)、在什麼情況下契約將失效等注意事項與聯絡方式。

● 保證書的資訊依以下順序列出：產品名稱、簽約日、保固期間、保固服務開始日、保固服務的內容、在什麼情況下保固有效或無效、聯絡方式。

 Point 2 注意使用說明書的正確使用方式、使用步驟！

正確的使用方式與使用步驟以條列方式標示。

 Point 3 留意最後的注意事項 (note) 及有 not 的句子！

文章最後寫有使用時的注意事項，以及導致保固失效的例子。

中譯　　　　　　　　你的新冰箱：使用說明書

拆封你的新冰箱後，請依以下指示操作：

● 插上電源線：
• 冰箱控制設定為 4。
• 維持該狀態 24 小時，待冷藏室及冷凍庫的溫度穩定了，再調整溫度。

● 如果冰箱溫度太高或太低，請利用 + 或 − 調高或調低冷凍庫或冷藏室的溫度。兩隔室的溫度控制範圍都是 1（溫度最高）到 7（溫度最低）。

● 請注意：改變其中一個隔室的溫度會影響另一個隔室的溫度。

● 只要其中一扇門開啟超過五分鐘，警示音就會響起；警示音響起時，每隔幾秒會響一次，直到冰箱門關閉為止。

任何因不當安裝所引起的損壞不在保固範圍內。如果不確定該如何正確安裝你的新冰箱，請致電客服尋求技術支援。

請撥打免付費電話 1-800-555-5687，詢問我們專業的客服技師。

1　與保證書、契約有效期限有關的題目
有效期限很常考，也很常使用換句話說的方式，例如將 two years 改寫成 24 months，必須注意。

題目

- How long is the contract valid for?（這份契約的有效期間多久？）
- What period of time does the warranty cover?（這份保證書的保固期間多久？）

文中的表達方式

- Contract Term: Two years / 24 months（契約期間：兩年 / 24 個月）
- World Electronics guarantees its products for a period of three years from the date of purchase.（世界電子為旗下產品提供自購買日起三年的保固服務。）
- Every camera in Sydney Camera comes with a 2-year warranty.
  （雪梨相機公司每一台相機都有兩年保固。）

2　與契約、保固失效以及注意事項有關的題目
通常可根據契約或保證書中有 not、only 的句子導出正確答案。

題目

- What is NOT covered by the (contract/warranty/guarantee)?
  （〔契約 / 保證書 / 保證〕的保固範圍不包含哪一項？）

文中的表達方式

- This unit should not be cleaned under running water.
  （本產品不得於流水下沖洗。）
- This warranty does not cover breakages caused by incorrect use of the product.
  （本保證書的保固範圍不包含因不當使用產品所引起的損壞。）
- Any damage to the microwave oven caused by previous neglect or improper handling of the microwave oven by customer will not be covered.
  （任何因顧客疏忽或不當使用微波爐所導致的損壞，皆不在保固範圍內。）
- Use of any attachments or filters other than Alpine HEPA type replacement filters may damage the device and will not be covered by the warranty.
  （更換時若使用非 Alpine HEPA 種類的零件或濾網，可能會損害設備，且不在保固範圍內。）

- The warranty is not valid when the item has been dropped or affected by liquids or battery leakage.
（因掉落或因液體、電池漏液所造成之損壞，不在本保證書的保固範圍內。）
- This warranty is valid only in the United States.（保固範圍僅限於美國。）
- All repairs should be performed by qualified personnel only.
（所有維修僅能由合格人員進行。）
- Never try to fix your own microwave. If it fails to work properly, always send it to an independent service center approved by our company.
（絕對不要試圖自己修理微波爐。如果微波爐無法正常運作，請送到本公司認可之獨立服務中心。）

加分表現

★ 與契約、保固失效以及注意事項有關的題目，答案通常如下

1. Damage due to <u>improper care</u>（因不當維護導致的損壞）
2. Malfunction caused by <u>negligence</u>（因疏忽導致的故障）
3. The <u>warranty</u> is valid only if you use the <u>approved parts</u>.
（保固僅限於使用認可之零件。）

★ 出現在產品說明書、保證書中關於故障、損壞的關鍵字

- approved parts 認可的零件
- be authorized by... 由…授權
- defective/faulty product 瑕疵產品
- invalid 形 無效的
- warranty 名 保證書
- malfunction 名 故障
- approved repair facility 認可的維修機構
- contract term 契約期間
- improper handling 不當使用
- valid 形 有效的
- guarantee 動 名 保證
- negligence 名 疏忽

Questions **1-3** refer to the following contract.

BRITANNIA HEATING AND COOLING INC.
329 Maple Lane
York

SERVICE MAINTENANCE CONTRACT

SERVICE ORDER	087123
Contract Date	October 23
Contract Term	12 months
Day that Service Begins	November 1

Purchaser	David White
Address	Colby Manor
	24, Cornish Way, York

Equipment's name	Ralston Furnace # 3751

Conditions of service. Technicians shall be responsible for

- Monthly check of gas pipes and heating elements
- Every six months changing of furnace filter
- Annual cleaning of vents throughout residence
- Monthly monitoring of heat and temperature levels
- Repair or replacement of any damaged parts

Note: Any damage to furnace caused by previous neglect or improper handling of furnace by customer will not be covered.

1. How long is the contract valid for?

    (A) One day

    (B) One month

    (C) Six months

    (D) One year

2. What is this maintenance contract for?

    (A) An air conditioner

    (B) A water filter

    (C) A home heating system

    (D) A kitchen stove

3. What is NOT covered by the maintenance contract?

    (A) Damage due to improper care

    (B) Cleaning of furnace vents

    (C) Checking of temperature settings

    (D) Repair of broken parts

DAY 8

說明書、契約、保證書

中譯 問題 1-3：請看以下契約。

不列顛尼亞溫控公司
約克郡楓樹巷 329 號

服務維修契約

服務代號	087123
簽約日期	10 月 23 日
[1]契約期間	12 個月
服務起始日	11 月 1 日
購買者	大衛·懷特
地址	約克郡康尼什路 24 號 科比莊園
[2]設備名稱	羅爾斯頓暖爐 #3751

服務條款。技師應負責：
◆ 每月檢查瓦斯管線和[2]加熱零件
◆ 每六個月更換暖氣濾網
◆ 每年清理全屋的排氣孔
◆ 每月監測熱度和溫度值
◆ 修理或更換任何受損零件

注意：[3]任何因顧客疏忽或不當使用暖爐所導致的損壞，皆不在保固範圍內。

單字
- □ maintenance 名 維修，保養
- □ purchaser 名 購買者
- □ manor 名 莊園
- □ furnace 名 暖爐
- □ technician 名 技師
- □ filter 名 濾網
- □ vent 名 排氣孔，通風孔
- □ repair 名 修理，修繕
- □ replacement 名 更換
- □ cover 動 適用

1. 這份契約的有效期間多久？
(A) 一天
(B) 一個月
(C) 六個月
(D) 一年

解說 找出 Contract Term　難易度 ★

從 Contract Term（契約期間）的 12 months（12個月）可知，契約的有效期限為一年，因此正確答案是 (D) One year。

換句話說　正文 12 months ➡ 選項 One year

2. 這份維修契約是針對什麼而訂定的？
(A) 空調
(B) 濾水器
(C) 家用暖氣系統
(D) 廚房爐具

解說 找出 Equipment's name　難易度 ★★

從 Equipment's name（設備名稱）的 Ralston Furnace #3751（羅爾斯頓暖爐 #3751）可知，契約中提到的設備是暖爐，也就是暖氣系統，因此正確答案是 (C) A home heating system。就算不知道 furnace 的意思，也可以從服務條款第一項的 heating elements（加熱零件）來判斷。

3. 維修契約的保固範圍不包含哪一項？
(A) 因不當維護造成的損壞
(B) 清理暖爐排氣孔
(C) 檢查溫度設定
(D) 修理損壞零件

解說 注意 Note　難易度 ★★

契約最後的 Note（注意）部分寫 Any damage to furnace caused by previous neglect or improper handling of furnace by customer will not be covered.（任何因顧客疏忽或不當使用暖爐所導致的損壞，皆不在保固範圍內。）也就是說，不當使用所造成的損壞不在保固範圍內，當然也包含不當維護在內，因此正確答案是 (A) Damage due to improper care。

換句話說　正文 improper handling ➡ 選項 improper care

Questions **1-3** refer to the following warranty.

Product Warranty

OmTech Electronics guarantees its products for a period of two years from the date of purchase. If any defect due to faulty materials or faulty manufacturing occurs within this period, the company will repair or replace the product at its own expense.

This warranty is only valid if convincing proof is provided, through a sales receipt or other official record, that the day on which service is claimed is within the guarantee period.

This warranty does not cover breakage caused by incorrect use of the product. The user should strictly follow all directions included in the Instructions for Use and should avoid any actions or uses that are described as undesired or which are warned against.

The guarantee does not cover damage which is the result of repair or alterations that have been carried out by persons not authorized by OmTech Electronics.

---

1. What period of time does the warranty cover?

    (A) One year
    (B) Two years
    (C) Ten years
    (D) A lifetime

2. What document should the customer provide in order to receive free repair?

    (A) A purchase receipt
    (B) An instruction manual
    (C) A service contract
    (D) A written guarantee

3. What action is NOT stated as making the warranty invalid?

    (A) Incorrectly using the product
    (B) Use of the product by a new owner
    (C) Altering the product oneself
    (D) Having a local repair shop fix the product

中譯 問題 1-3：請看以下保證書。

產品保證書

歐姆科技電子為旗下產品提供[1]自購買日起兩年的保固服務。在此期間，若有任何因材料不良或製造問題所造成的瑕疵，本公司將會免費維修或更換產品。

本保證書僅在[2]提供有效憑證（如銷售收據或其他正式紀錄），證明送修日仍在保固期間內時方能生效。

本保證書的保固範圍不包含[3]因不當使用產品所造成的損壞。使用者應嚴格遵守使用說明書中的所有指示，並避免任何說明書中列為不當或警告的行為或使用方式。

[3]由非歐姆科技電子授權之人員維修或更換零件所造成的損壞，不在保固範圍內。

單字

□ date of purchase 購買日
□ at one's own expense 自費
□ convincing 形 令人信服的
□ claim 動 要求
□ breakage 名 損壞，破損

□ strictly 副 嚴格地
□ undesired 形 不建議的，不當的
□ warn 動 警告
□ alteration 名 改造，變更
□ carry out... 進行…

1. 這份保證書的保固期間多久？
(A) 一年
(B) 兩年
(C) 十年
(D) 終身

解說　注意數字　（難易度）★

從第一段第一句 OmTech Electronics guarantees its products for a period of two years from the date of purchase.（歐姆科技電子為旗下產品提供自購買日起兩年的保固服務。）可知，保固期限為兩年，因此正確答案是 (B) Two years。

2. 若想獲得免費維修，顧客應提供什麼文件？
(A) 購買收據
(B) 使用手冊
(C) 服務契約
(D) 手寫保證書

解說　注意什麼狀況下保固有效 (valid) 和有 only 的句子　（難易度）★

從保證書第二段的 This warranty is only valid if convincing proof is provided, through a sales receipt or other official record,...（本保證書僅在提供有效憑證〔如銷售收據或其他正式紀錄〕，……方能生效。）可知，必須提供如購買收據的有效憑證才能獲得免費維修，因此正確答案是 (A) A purchase receipt。

換句話說　正文 sales receipt ➡ 選項 purchase receipt

3. 哪一項行為不會使保固失效？
(A) 不當使用產品
(B) 由新主人使用產品
(C) 自己改造產品
(D) 找當地的修理店修理產品

解說　NOT 問句通常可用消去法解題
（難易度）★★★

保證書最後兩段提及導致保固失效的要素，包含第三段的 breakage caused by incorrect use of the product（因不當使用產品所造成的損壞），以及第四段的 damage which is the result of repair or alterations that have been carried out by persons not authorized by OmTech Electronics（由非歐姆科技電子授權之人員維修或更換零件所造成的損壞），分別與 (A)、(C)、(D) 相符，沒有提到的是 (B) Use of the product by a new owner，為正確答案。

Questions 1-3 refer to the following instructions.

Digital Thermometer: Instructions for Care and Use

The average body temperature ranges from 97.0°F (36.1°C) to 99.0°F (37.2°C) depending upon the individual. The generally accepted "normal" temperature is 98.6°F (37°C). Usually, each person's body temperature is lower in the morning than in the afternoon. In addition, temperature will differ depending upon where you take your temperature. If you place the thermometer under your arm, the temperature it records will be 1 degree °F (0.5°C) lower than if placed underneath your tongue. In either case, your temperature should be taken when you are stationary: either sitting down or standing up.

Following are the instructions for use:

- Do not walk, run, or talk during temperature taking.
- Clean the thermometer before and after each use.
- Store the unit in its protective case when not in use.
- Do not bite the thermometer tip.
- Do not store the unit where it will be exposed to direct sunlight, dust, or high temperatures.
- Do not attempt to disassemble the unit, except to replace the battery.

1. What do the instructions say about body temperature?

    (A) It varies during the day.
    (B) It is the same for each individual.
    (C) It is higher in the morning.
    (D) It should be taken only while sitting.

2. What condition is NOT mentioned as harmful to the thermometer during storage?

    (A) Sunlight
    (B) Humidity
    (C) Dirt
    (D) Heat

3. According to the instructions, when can the thermometer be taken apart?

    (A) When re-setting the temperature
    (B) When cleaning it
    (C) When changing the battery
    (D) When repairing it

中譯 問題 1-3：請看以下使用說明。

數位體溫計：維護及使用說明

體溫因人而異，平均落在華氏 97 度（攝氏 36.1 度）至華氏 99 度（攝氏 37.2 度）之間。一般可接受的「正常」體溫為華氏 98.6 度（攝氏 37 度）。[1]通常每個人早上的體溫會低於午後。此外，體溫也會因測量的位置而有不同。如果你將體溫計置於腋下，測量出來的溫度會比置於舌下時低華氏 1 度（攝氏 0.5 度）。不管置於腋下或舌下，測量體溫時都必須是靜止的狀態，坐著或站著都可以。

以下為使用說明：
- 測量體溫時請勿走路、奔跑或說話。
- 每次使用前後請清潔體溫計。
- 未使用時請將體溫計存放於保護盒中。
- 請勿咬體溫計的尖端。
- [2]體溫計不可直接曝曬於陽光下，也不得暴露於灰塵和高溫中。
- [3]除更換電池外，請勿試圖拆解體溫計。

單字

□ thermometer 名 溫度計	□ be in use 使用中
□ range 動（在一定範圍內）變化	□ protective 形 保護的
□ individual 名 個人，個體	□ case 名 盒，箱
□ differ 動 不同	□ tip 名 尖端
□ stationary 形 靜止不動的	□ be exposed to... 暴露於…
□ store 動 保管，存放	□ disassemble 動 拆開，拆解

解答 **1.** (A) **2.** (B) **3.** (C)

1. 關於體溫，這份使用說明提到了
什麼？
(A) 一天之中會有變化。
(B) 每個人的體溫都一樣。
(C) 早上比較高。
(D) 只能坐著測量。

解說 找出 body temperature　(難易度) ★★

從使用說明第三句 Usually, each person's body temperature is lower in the morning than in the afternoon.（通常每個人早上的體溫會低於午後。）可知，體溫在一天之中會有變化，因此正確答案是 (A) It varies during the day.。

---

2. 關於存放時對體溫計有害的要素，
文中未提及哪一項？
(A) 陽光
(B) 溼氣
(C) 灰塵
(D) 高溫

解說 NOT 問句通常可用消去法解題
(難易度) ★

從使用說明條列第五點 Do not store the unit where it will be exposed to direct sunlight, dust, or high temperatures.（體溫計不可直接曝曬於陽光下，也不得暴露於灰塵和高溫中。）可知，陽光、灰塵或高溫的環境皆不利於體溫計的保存。文中沒有提到溼氣，因此正確答案是 (B) Humidity。

換句話說	正文 dust ➡ 選項 Dirt
	正文 high temperatures ➡ 選項 Heat

3. 根據使用說明的內容，什麼時候可
以拆開體溫計？
(A) 重設溫度時
(B) 清潔時
(C) 換電池時
(D) 修理時

解說 注意使用說明的條列部分和有 not 的
句子　(難易度) ★

從使用說明條列部分的最後一點 Do not attempt to disassemble the unit, except to replace the battery.（除更換電池外，請勿試圖拆解體溫計。）可知，換電池時可以拆解體溫計，因此正確答案是 (C) When changing the battery。

換句話說	正文 replace ➡ 選項 changing

1 分鐘 CHECK!

複習「說明書、契約、保證書」的閱讀重點及 Day 8 的必背字彙。

「說明書、契約、保證書」的閱讀重點

- ☐ 電子產品操作說明書、服務維修契約、保證書很常考。
- ☐ 可從標題掌握產品名稱，並知道這是說明書、契約或保證書。閱讀時注意這三者各自的格式。
- ☐ 正確的使用方式、使用步驟通常以條列方式表示。
- ☐ 注意事項、產品的保固在什麼狀況下失效等，有 not 的句子很容易被問到，必須注意。

「說明書、契約、保證書」的必背字彙

- ☐ use and care guide 使用說明書
- ☐ please follow these directions 請遵守以下的使用說明
- ☐ improper 形 不當的
- ☐ not covered by warranty 不在保固範圍內
- ☐ equipment 名 設備
- ☐ valid 形 有效的
- ☐ guarantee 動 名 保證
- ☐ date of purchase 購買日
- ☐ breakage 名 損壞，破損
- ☐ incorrect use 不正確的使用
- ☐ repair 動 名 修理，修繕
- ☐ be in use 使用中
- ☐ maintenance 名 維修，保養
- ☐ disassemble 動 拆開，拆解

Day 9

本日主題
● 多篇文章測驗

多篇文章測驗分為雙篇文章測驗與三篇文章測驗兩種題型。雙篇文章測驗是讀完兩篇相關的文章（如：「客訴」與「道歉」的電子郵件）後回答五個問題，三篇文章測驗則是讀完三篇相關的文章（如：「徵才廣告」與「求職信」、「履歷表」），之後回答五個問題。

解題方式基本上與 Day 1 到 Day 8 學過的單篇文章測驗相同，不過如果先看過題目，可判斷哪些題目屬於讀完其中一篇文章就能夠解題的「一篇文章型」，哪些屬於必須讀完兩篇文章的「兩篇文章型」，哪些又是必須讀完所有文章才能夠導出答案的「三篇文章型」，藉此加快閱讀速度。

以下是摘自實際測驗的短文，請翻到 p. 148，看看會出哪些題目吧。

● 文章 1

HELP WANTED

London Apparel is a multinational company based in Ottawa and expanding into Northeast Asia. We are seeking a regional manager for Asian sales. The position will be based in Tokyo and the successful candidate will oversee the firm's branch operations in Seoul, Shanghai, and Osaka.

Qualifications

Bachelor's degree or higher required
At least 5 years of sales experience at a managerial level (preferably in retail fashion) necessary
Native speaker level of English essential
Fluency in Japanese required
Understanding of Asian cultures a must
Basic Chinese or Korean language skills a plus

Compensation and benefits

- Competitive salary based on previous experience
- Full health plan
- Subsidized housing in serviced apartment
- Expense account for travel

To apply, send résumé with 3 references to humanresources@londonapparel.com

---

● 文章 2

TO: humanresources@londonapparel.com
FROM: jgarcia@hmail.com
DATE: June 14
SUBJECT: Application for your regional manager for Asian sales position

Dear Human Resources Department of London Apparel,

I would like to apply for your recently advertised position of regional manager for Asian sales. I have more than five years of experience as district sales manager for the Canadian casual clothing retailer "The Jeans Company" overseeing sales and marketing throughout Western Canada. Prior to that I was for four years the manager of a newly established flagship store of Globalfashion in Beijing. Before that, I worked in sales for Globalfashion in Canada. In addition, when in university, I lived for a year in Osaka and was an exchange student at Osaka University.

Kindly see my attached résumé. I am very interested in this position with your firm and available for an interview, in person or by Skype, at your convenience.

Very truly yours,

Johnny Garcia

● 文章 3

Résumé

Johnny Garcia (jgarcia@hmail.com)

1345 Maple Lane, Vancouver, Canada

Tel. 1-604-334-5643

Education: B.A. in Business, Minor in Chinese. University of Calgary, Alberta, 2005

Experience:

- District Sales Manager 2012-present, The Jeans Company, Vancouver, Canada
- Store Manager 2008-2012, Globalfashion, Beijing, China
- Assistant Sales Director, 2005-2008, Globalfashion, Toronto, Canada

Language Skills: Native speaker of English, fluent in Chinese, basic Japanese speaking ability

Point 1 看看常見的文章組合！

常考的組合是「客訴」與「道歉」的書信或電子郵件、「要求」與「回應」的書信或電子郵件、「新聞報導」與電子郵件及書信裡的「評論」，「表格」與「通知」，還有「徵才廣告」、「履歷表」與「電子郵件」等。釐清文章之間的關聯性，更容易判斷答案出現在哪一篇文章裡。

Point 2 先看題目！

先看題目，判斷是一篇文章型、兩篇文章型或三篇文章型的題目，藉此判斷必須閱讀文章的哪個部分。以 pp. 146-147 的文章為例，舉凡 What position is open?（哪個職務有空缺？）、Where is the headquarters located?（總公司位於何處？）等都屬於一篇文章型的題目，只要閱讀文章 1 的徵才廣告即可回答。至於 What required qualification does Johnny Garcia lack?（強尼‧賈西亞欠缺哪一項應徵的必要條件？）則是兩篇文章型的問題。詳細的判斷方式請見 STEP 2。

雙篇文章測驗的題目分成兩種：只需閱讀一篇文章，就能導出正確答案的一篇文章型題目，以及必須讀完兩篇文章，才能導出正確答案的兩篇文章型題目。三篇文章測驗則多了必須讀完三篇文章，才能導出正確答案的三篇文章型題目。我們以 pp. 146-147 的閱讀測驗為例，學習如何判斷。

 一篇文章型
這類題目最多。請快速判斷必須閱讀哪一篇文章的哪一個部分。

題目

● What position is being advertised?（廣告刊登的是什麼職缺？）

解說 題目問的是職缺，因此判斷只要看文章 1 的徵才廣告就能找到答案。從第二句 We are seeking a regional manager for Asian sales.（我們正在尋找一位負責亞洲業務的區域經理。）可知，該公司要找的是業務經理，因此正確答案是 Sales manager（業務經理）。

● Where is London Apparel's global headquarters located?
（倫敦服裝公司的全球總部位於何處？）

解說 題目問的是總部的所在地，只要看文章 1 的徵才廣告就能找出答案。從第一句 London Apparel is a multinational company based in Ottawa...（倫敦服裝公司是一家跨國公司，總部位於渥太華……）可知，總部位於渥太華，因此正確答案是 It is located in Ottawa.（位於渥太華。）

● What does Mr. Garcia offer to do?（賈西亞先生表示願意做什麼？）

解說 題目問的是求職者賈西亞對於徵才廣告的回覆，因此判斷只要看文章 2 的電子郵件就能找到答案。文章最後一段提到 I am very interested ... and available for an interview,...（我非常感興趣……也可以接受面試……），可知賈西亞願意接受面試，因此正確答案是 Participate in an interview（參加面試）。

2 兩篇文章型
五個題目中大約會出一到兩題。要確實掌握文章的組合。

● What requirement does Mr. Garcia appear to lack?
（賈西亞先生看起來欠缺哪一項應徵的必要條件？）

解說 題目問的是賈西亞所欠缺的應徵的必要條件，因此要看文章 1 的徵才廣告上的資格條件 (Qualifications) 和文章 3 的履歷表。資格條件的部分提及 Fluency in Japanese required（日文需達流利程度），而履歷表的語言能力 (Language Skills) 則提到 basic Japanese speaking ability（基本日文對話能力），與徵才條件不符，因此正確答案是 Japanese fluency（日文流利）。

● What does Mr. Garcia's application appear to lack?
（賈西亞先生的應徵資料看起來缺少什麼？）

解說 題目問的是賈西亞的應徵資料所缺少的東西，因此要看文章 1 的徵才廣告和文章 2 的電子郵件。徵才廣告最後提到 To apply, send résumé with 3 references to...（應徵者請將履歷表及三封推薦信寄至……），但電子郵件裡只寫了 Kindly see my attached résumé.（懇請參考附件履歷表。）未提到隨信附上三封推薦信，因此正確答案是 References（推薦信）。

DAY
9

多篇文章測驗

題目

● What is likely Mr. Garcia's most attractive qualification for this position?
（就這個職缺來說，賈西亞先生最吸引人的資格條件是什麼？）

解說 從文章 1 的徵才廣告第一段可知，該公司要招募亞洲區的業務經理，資格條件也提及 Understanding of Asian cultures a must（需了解亞洲文化）。文章 2 的電子郵件與文章 3 的履歷表都提到賈西亞曾在 Beijing（北京）擔任經理，電子郵件也提到他曾是 Osaka University（大阪大學）的交換學生，履歷表中更提到 fluent in Chinese（中文流利）。由此可知，他在亞洲的求學、求職經驗是最吸引人之處，因此正確答案是 His experience in Asia（他在亞洲的經歷）。

中譯　　　　　　　　　　　　　　　徵人啓事

倫敦服裝公司是一家跨國公司，總部位於渥太華，後擴張至東北亞。我們正在尋找一位負責亞洲業務的區域經理。這個職位的工作地點在東京，錄取者將負責管理公司於首爾、上海和大阪分店的營運。

資格條件

學士學位或以上
需有至少五年管理階層的業務經驗（零售業更佳）
英語需達母語程度
日文需達流利程度
需了解亞洲文化
具中文或韓文基礎為佳

薪酬及福利

● 具有競爭力的待遇（依經歷而定）
● 完整的健康計畫
● 酒店式公寓的住屋補貼
● 差旅費用補助

應徵者請將履歷表及三封推薦信寄至 humanresources@londonapparel.com。

收件人：humanresources@londonapparel.com
寄件人：jgarcia@hmail.com
日期：6 月 14 日
主旨：應徵貴公司亞洲業務區域經理一職

親愛的倫敦服裝公司人力資源部：

我想應徵貴公司近日刊登的亞洲業務區域經理一職。我在加拿大休閒服飾零售商「珍氏公司」擔任區域業務經理超過五年，負責管理加拿大西部的業務及行銷。在此之前，我在北京全球時尚公司當初新開幕的旗艦店，擔任了四年的經理。在那之前，我則是加拿大全球時尚公司的業務。此外，大學時，我曾在大阪住過一年，是大阪大學的交換學生。

懇請參考附件履歷表。我對貴公司這個職缺非常感興趣，也可以依您方便，接受面對面或透過 SKYPE 的面試。

強尼‧賈西亞
敬上

履歷表
強尼‧賈西亞 (jgarcia@hmail.com)
加拿大溫哥華楓樹巷 1345 號
電話：1-604-334-5643
學歷：亞伯達卡加利大學商業學士，副修中文，2005 年畢業

經歷：
● 區域業務經理，2012 年至今，加拿大溫哥華珍氏公司
● 店經理，2008 年至 2012 年，中國北京全球時尚公司
● 業務副主任，2005 年至 2008 年，加拿大多倫多全球時尚公司
語言能力：英文為母語，中文流利，基本日文對話能力

Questions 1-5 refer to the following notice and letter.

PeopleCare Insurance
Policy number: 456543

INSURANCE RENEWAL NOTICE

Your present auto insurance policy will expire on February 20. You should renew your policy as soon as possible to avoid a lapse in coverage.

Based upon the following information, the total cost of a six-month policy to insure your vehicle is $315.

Insured vehicle: Model: 4-door Grand Prix Luxury Sedan
Maker: Heartland Motors
Estimated current value: $14,999

Choose your payment option.

Your 3 options	Pay now	Discount savings	Your total cost
Pay in full now (for maximum savings)	$229.00	$86.00	$229.00
Pay in three installments	$93.67	$34.00	$281.00
Pay in six installments	$52.50	$0.00	$315.00

Please enclose your check for the option you have selected. Do NOT include cash.

If you have any questions, please write to Customer Assistance, PeopleCare Insurance, 2971 Office Park, Suite 24, Newark, NJ.

Sally Nix
243 Elm Street
Ridgewood, NJ

February 1

Customer Assistance
PeopleCare Insurance
2971 Office Park, Suite 24
Newark, NJ

Dear Customer Service Agents,

I am writing to point out to you an error in the renewal notice I recently received. You have incorrectly recorded some of the information about my car. Here is the correct description:

Model: 2-door Grand Am Compact
Maker: Heartland Motors
Estimated current value: $12,000

I suspect the correct information will significantly lower the premium due.

I am enclosing your requested premium payment with this letter of inquiry to avoid any gap in coverage. However, I would like you to re-calculate my premium and reimburse me for any overpayment.

Sincerely yours,
Sally Nix
Sally Nix

Encl: Payment in full

1. What payment option is NOT available?

(A) One complete payment
(B) Two partial payments
(C) Three partial payments
(D) Six partial payments

2. What data about the car may the insurance company have incorrectly stated?

(A) The owner of the auto
(B) The car manufacturer
(C) The type of auto
(D) The vehicle manufacturing date

3. What has Ms. Nix included with her letter?

(A) A copy of her driver's license
(B) A personal check
(C) The record of her credit card payment
(D) The original sales receipt for her car

4. What is indicated about Ms. Nix?

(A) She will purchase a different vehicle.
(B) She will increase her insurance coverage.
(C) She will change insurers.
(D) She will receive some money back.

5. In the letter, the word "premium" in paragraph 2, line 1, is closest in meaning to

(A) special service
(B) additional request
(C) insurance fee
(D) transportation fare

練習題 **1** 答案與解說

中譯 問題 1-5：請看以下通知和信件。

顧民保險

保單號碼：456543

保險續保通知

您現在的汽車保險將於 2 月 20 日到期。您應盡快續保，以免保險期間無法銜接。

根據以下資訊，您汽車的六個月保險費用共為 315 美元。

保險車輛：[2] 車款：四門格蘭瑞斯豪華轎車
　　　　　　製造商：哈特蘭汽車
　　　　　　估計現值：14,999 美元

請選擇付款方案。

[1] 您的三種方案	現在支付	折扣金額	總支出
現在全額支付（最省錢）	$229.00	$86.00	$229.00
分三期支付	$93.67	$34.00	$281.00
分六期支付	$52.50	$0.00	$315.00

[3] 請依所選方案附上支票，勿使用現金。

如果您有任何疑問，請寫信至新澤西紐華克辦公園區 2971 號 24 號室，顧民保險客戶協助部收。

單字

- □ policy 名 保單，保險
- □ lapse 名 失效
- □ coverage 名 保險給付範圍
- □ insure 動 為…投保
- □ sedan 名 轎車
- □ estimated current value 估計現值
- □ option 名 選擇，選項
- □ pay in installments 分期付款

莎莉・尼克斯
新澤西里基伍德
榆木街 243 號

2 月 1 日

顧民保險客戶協助部
新澤西紐華克
辦公園區 2971 號 24 號室

親愛的客服專員：

這封信是為了告知我最近收到的續保通知內容有誤，我的車輛資訊有部分紀錄不正確。以下是正確的資訊：

²車款：雙門葛蘭美小型汽車
製造商：哈特蘭汽車
估計現值：12,000 美元

我想正確的資訊會大幅減低我應支付的⁵保費。

³隨信附上貴公司所要求的保費，以免保險期間中斷。但是，⁴我希望貴公司能重新計算我的保費，並將所有溢付的保費退還給我。

莎莉・尼克斯
莎莉・尼克斯
敬上

附件：保費全額

DAY
9

多篇文章測驗

單字

□ compact 名 小型車
□ suspect 動 猜想
□ premium 名 保費
□ inquiry 名 詢問

□ gap 名 空白，間斷
□ re-calculate 動 重新計算
□ reimburse A for B 將 B 的款項退還給 A

1. (B) **2.** (C) **3.** (B) **4.** (D) **5.** (C)

1. 未提供哪一種付款方案？
  (A) 一次付清
  (B) 分兩期付款
  (C) 分三期付款
  (D) 分六期付款

解說 找出 payment option   （難易度）★★

通知裡的 payment option（付款方案）列出了三種方案：Pay in full（全額支付）、Pay in three installments（分三期支付）、Pay in six installments（分六期支付），分別和選項 (A)、(C)、(D) 相符。文中沒有提到分兩期付款，因此正確答案是 (B) Two partial payments。

---

2. 保險公司可能把汽車的什麼資訊寫錯了？
  (A) 車主
  (B) 汽車製造商
  (C) 汽車類型
  (D) 汽車製造日期

解說 兩篇文章型 找出與汽車有關的內容
（難易度）★★

對照通知的 Insured vehicle（保險車輛）與信件的 Here is the correct description（以下是正確的資訊）後可知，通知提到的車款是 4-door Grand Prix Luxury Sedan（四門格蘭瑞斯豪華轎車），信件提到的車款是 2-door Grand Am Compact（雙門葛蘭美小型汽車），也就是說車子的種類不同，因此正確答案是 (C) The type of auto。

---

3. 尼克斯小姐在信中附上了什麼？
  (A) 她的駕照影本
  (B) 個人支票
  (C) 信用卡的付款紀錄
  (D) 購車收據的正本

解說 兩篇文章型 注意通知裡表格以外的內容，並閱讀尼克斯的信 （難易度）★★

從通知裡表格下方的 Please enclose your check...（請附上支票……）可知，保險公司要求以支票付款。而從信件最後一段的 I am enclosing your requested premium payment...（隨信附上貴公司所要求的保費……）可知，支付保費用的支票連同信件一起寄出，因此正確答案是 (B) A personal check。

4. 關於尼克斯小姐，文中提到了什麼？

(A) 她將購買不同的汽車。
(B) 她將增加她的保險額度。
(C) 她將更換保險公司。
(D) 她將收到一些退款。

解說 注意書信的版面格式和表示要求的關鍵句　(難易度) ★★

從信件最後一句 However, I would like you to re-calculate my premium and reimburse me for any overpayment.（但是，我希望貴公司能重新計算我的保費，並將所有溢付的保費退還給我。）可知，尼克斯小姐要求保險公司退回溢付的保費，也就是說她將收到一些退款，因此正確答案是 (D) She will receive some money back.。

換句話說　正文 reimburse me for any overpayment
➡ 選項 receive some money back

5. 在信件中，第二段第一行的單字 premium，最接近哪一個意思？

(A) 特別服務
(B) 額外要求
(C) 保險費用
(D) 運輸費用

解說 從前後文判斷特定語句的意思　(難易度) ★★

信件第一段提及車子的估計現值，與通知裡所寫的估計現值有落差。合理推測，車子的估計現值愈低，保費就會愈低，因此第二段第一行的 premium 應是保費的意思，正確答案是 (C) insurance fee。

Questions 1-5 refer to the following announcement, schedule and e-mail.

Strategic Planning Meeting
Sponsored by the Sales and Marketing Department
Seminar Room 2
Monday, December 10

To assist the research & development (R&D) team in planning new products, the sales and marketing department will organize a series of workshops and presentations discussing emerging trends in software design. See the attached schedule for details.

If you have any questions or suggestions to make the meeting better, you are welcome to e-mail Mary Baker, executive secretary, Sales & Marketing (mbaker@softwareinc.com) and please cc Isaac Silver, Strategic Planning (isilver@softwareinc.com).

Please consult your department head to confirm whether you are required to attend.

Meeting Schedule: Monday, December 10

9:00 A.M. - 9:30 A.M.	Coffee, Opening remarks, Staff introductions	Carla Francis, sales manager
10:00 A.M. - 10:45 A.M.	SESSION 1	Current applications for smart phones Antonio Christakos, software designer
10:45 A.M. - 11:00 A.M.	Q & A	
11:00 A.M. - 11:45 A.M.	SESSION 2	Music, video, photo software in the planning stages Isaac Silver, strategic planner
11:45 A.M. - 12:00 noon	Q & A	
12:00 noon - 1:00 P.M.	Catered lunch, small group discussion	
1:00 P.M. - 1:45 P.M.	SESSION 3	What the customers might want Vi Kanokawan, director of marketing research
1:45 P.M. - 2:00 P.M.	Q & A	
2:00 P.M. - 2:30 P.M.	SESSION 4	Open discussion: Brainstorming for the future All attendees

TO: Mary Baker <mbaker@softwareinc.com>

CC: Isaac Silver <isilver@softwareinc.com>

FROM: Phil Johnson <pjohnson@softwareinc.com>

Dear Mary,

I want to thank you and your colleagues for your hard work in organizing the upcoming Strategic Planning Meeting. However, I have a couple of suggestions to make the event even better.

First, we need to know what our competitors are doing. Would it be possible for someone in marketing to give us a brief presentation on what other products and services firms like ours are planning at the moment? This would probably mean an extra session.

Next, I think we need to expand the final roundtable discussion that everyone participates in. This is the part of the meeting that is likely to generate the most important ideas. It should be at least doubled.

Otherwise, the scheduled sessions look terrific. I look forward to attending.

Phil
Phil Johnson, senior researcher

DAY
9

多篇文章測驗

1. Who is responsible for planning the meeting?

   (A) The research & development team
   (B) The product design division
   (C) The sales and marketing department
   (D) The marketing research group

2. When does the meeting begin?

   (A) At 9:00 A.M.
   (B) At 10:00 A.M.
   (C) At 10:45 A.M.
   (D) At 11:00 A.M.

3. Who will most likely talk about products now being developed?

   (A) Carla Francis
   (B) Antonio Christakos
   (C) Isaac Silver
   (D) Vi Kanokawan

4. What topic does Mr. Johnson suggest should be added?

   (A) The plans of rival firms
   (B) The cost of current research
   (C) The state of smart phone design
   (D) The need for better communication

5. What current session may be increased in length?

   (A) Session 1
   (B) Session 2
   (C) Session 3
   (D) Session 4

中譯 問題 1-5：請看以下公告、時程表和電子郵件。

策略計畫會議
[1]業務行銷部主辦
2 號講座室
12 月 10 日星期一

為協助研發團隊開發新產品，業務行銷部將安排一系列工作坊和演講，討論軟體設計的新興趨勢。詳情請見附件的時程表。

如果你有任何疑問，或可以讓會議更加完善的建議，歡迎寄電子郵件給業務行銷部的執行祕書瑪麗‧貝克 (mbaker@softwareinc.com)，並請同時副件給策略計畫部的艾薩克‧西爾弗 (isilver@softwareinc.com)。

請詢問所屬的部門主管，確認你是否需要出席。

單字

□ strategic planning 策略計畫
□ organize 動 安排，組織
□ emerging 形 新興的

□ trend 名 趨勢，走向
□ executive 形 執行的
□ consult 動 詢問，請教

會議時程表：12 月 10 日星期一

[2]早上 9:00-9:30	咖啡時間、開幕致詞、員工介紹	業務經理 卡拉‧法蘭西斯
早上 10:00-10:45	場次 1	智慧型手機現有的應用程式 軟體設計師 安東尼奧‧克萊斯塔科斯
早上 10:45-11:00	問答時間	
早上 11:00-11:45	場次 2	[3]研發階段的音樂、影像和照相軟體 策略計畫師 艾薩克‧西爾弗
早上 11:45- 中午 12:00	問答時間	
中午 12:00- 下午 1:00	外燴午餐，小組討論	
下午 1:00-1:45	場次 3	顧客可能想要什麼 市場研究主任 維‧卡諾卡旺
下午 1:45-2:00	問答時間	

下午 2:00-2:30	⁵場次 4	開放討論：關於未來的腦力激盪 所有出席者

收件人：瑪麗・貝克 <mbaker@softwareinc.com>
副件：艾薩克・西爾弗 <isilver@softwareinc.com>
寄件人：菲爾・強森 <pjohnson@softwareinc.com>

親愛的瑪麗：

我想謝謝你和你的同事，用心安排了即將到來的策略計畫會議。然而，我有一些建議可以讓這項活動更加完善。

⁴首先，我們必須知道我們的競爭者在做什麼。有沒有可能請行銷部的同事做個簡短的報告，告訴我們和我們同性質的公司目前正計畫推出其他哪些產品或服務？這或許意味著需要多安排一個場次。

⁵其次，我想我們需要將最後由所有人一起參與的圓桌討論給延長。這是整場會議中有可能激盪出最重要點子的部分，時間至少應該加倍。

除了以上兩點之外，規畫的場次看來好極了。我非常期待參與。

資深研究員 菲爾・強森
菲爾

DAY
9

多篇文章測驗

1. (C)　**2.** (A)　**3.** (C)　**4.** (A)　**5.** (D)

1. 這場會議由誰負責籌辦？
　(A) 研發團隊
　(B) 產品設計部
　(C) 業務行銷部
　(D) 市場研究團隊

解說　**注意公告的標題**　　難易度 ★★

從公告的標題下面的 Sponsored by the Sales and Marketing Department（業務行銷部主辦）可知，會議由業務行銷部主辦，因此正確答案是 (C) The sales and marketing department。

2. 會議什麼時候開始？
　(A) 早上 9:00
　(B) 早上 10:00
　(C) 早上 10:45
　(D) 早上 11:00

解說　**看時程表的時段**　　難易度 ★★

時程表的時段最上面一欄是 9:00 A.M.-9:30 A.M.（早上 9:00-9:30），可知會議早上 9 點開始，因此正確答案是 (A) At 9:00 A.M.。

3. 誰最有可能談到現在正在研發的產品？
　(A) 卡拉‧法蘭西斯
　(B) 安東尼奧‧克萊斯塔科斯
　(C) 艾薩克‧西爾弗
　(D) 維‧卡諾卡旺

解說　**看時程表，找出人名與內容**
難易度 ★★

從場次 2 的主題 Music, video, photo software in the planning stages（研發階段的音樂、影像和照相軟體）可知，該場次會談到還在研發階段的產品，而該時段由艾薩克‧西爾弗主講，因此正確答案是 (C) Isaac Silver。

4. 強森先生建議應該增加什麼主題？
　(A) 競爭公司的計畫
　(B) 近來研究的支出
　(C) 智慧型手機設計的狀況
　(D) 改善溝通之需求

解說　**注意電子郵件每一段的開頭**
難易度 ★★

強森先生是電子郵件的寄件人，所以要看電子郵件。從郵件第二段第一句 First, we need to know what our competitors are doing.（首先，我們必須知道我們的競爭者在做什麼。）可知，強森先生認為應該要知道競爭公司的計畫，因此正確答案是 (A) The plans of rival firms。

換句話說　正文 competitors ➡ 選項 rival firms

問題 1-5：請看以下信件、通知和電子郵件。

天堂飯店渡假村

卡米爾莊園：分時渡假村

棕櫚泉 CA 90588

狄塞爾路 1800 號

渡假村電話：(714) 555-0987

辦公室傳真：(714) 555-0986

3 月 7 日

預約確認
弗瑞德列克・福頓先生
聖地牙哥 CA 92120
布魯邁爾地 8199 號

預約號碼：#186879A
[3]抵達日：5 月 12 日
退房日：5 月 19 日
住宿天數：7 晚
住宿房型：雙床房

入住時間為下午 4:00
退房時間為早上 10:00

渡假村及房客資訊
請保留這份確認信，做為未來參考之用。[5]入住前 60 天內取消此預約將收取取消費，並可能導致未來的預約不被受理。

請確認所有成年的入住房客於入住時皆持有有效身分證件。[1]不管在什麼情況下皆不可延遲退房。早上 10:00 後退房將依渡假村的標準房價收取一天的住宿費。[1]渡假村內不允許寵物或過大的車輛進入。

所有特殊要求（如：高椅、折疊床等）必須於入住前至少 24 小時提出。關於今年夏天預定進行的渡假村整修與修繕一事，請重新檢視附件的通知，此通知在您上網預約時於網站上亦有提供。

預約櫃台
安妮塔・揚格
安妮塔・揚格

通知

今年春夏造訪卡米爾莊園渡假村的遊客會注意到，²渡假村內在進行住宿設施外部的修繕工程。這項工程將於白天分段進行，並於 7 月 15 日完成。渡假村內的正常活動將不受影響。

卡米爾莊園渡假村 經理

收件人：天堂飯店渡假村 <kamelestates@bus.net.com>
寄件人：弗瑞德列克‧福頓 <ffulton@psystems.com>
⁵日期：5 月 7 日
回覆：預約號碼 #186879A

致：預約櫃台 安妮塔‧揚格

³⁴⁵這封信是為了取消我於下週 5 月 12 日至 19 日的預約。重讀確認信時，我注意到在我們造訪期間將進行施工。這我沒辦法接受。我為這個分時渡假計畫付了大筆的年費，所以我期待我的年假應該是寧靜而祥和的。

稍晚我將和你聯絡，重新預約七月下旬的一週假期。

弗瑞德‧福頓

單字

□ take place 進行
□ unacceptable 形 無法接受的

□ annual fee 年費

解答 **1.** (B) **2.** (C) **3.** (C) **4.** (C) **5.** (B)

1. 卡米爾莊園渡假村的住宿須知中未禁止哪一項？
(A) 在渡假村内停放大型卡車
(B) 帶小孩過夜
(C) 在渡假村和寵物狗玩
(D) 延後退房時間

解說 看信件的 Resort & Guest Information；NOT 問句通常可用消去法解題　**難易度** ★ ★ ★

從信件的 Resort & Guest Information（渡假村及房客資訊）第二段第二句的 Late check-out is not permitted under any circumstances.（不管在什麼情況下皆不可延遲退房。）可知，渡假村不接受延遲退房。同一段最後一句是 No pets or oversized vehicles are allowed on the resort property.（渡假村内不允許寵物或過大的車輛進入。）表示不可帶寵物，也不能停放大型車輛。信中並沒有提及不能帶小孩過夜，因此正確答案是 (B) Staying overnight with small children。

2. 關於卡米爾莊園施工計畫的敘述，何者為真？
(A) 主要於晚上施工。
(B) 只要一個月就可以完成。
(C) 僅限於建築外部。
(D) 其設計在於擴大住宿設施的規模。

解說 看通知的内容　**難易度** ★ ★ ★

從通知第一句的 construction activity at the resort associated with repairs to the exterior of the guest accommodations（渡假村内在進行住宿設施外部的修繕工程）可知，修繕工程是針對建築外部，因此正確答案是 (C) It is limited to the outside of the buildings.。

換句話說　正文 the exterior of ➡ 選項 the outside of
正文 accommodations ➡ 選項 buildings

3. 福頓先生在卡米爾莊園的假期原本應該什麼時候開始？

(A) 3 月 7 日
(B) 5 月 7 日
(C) 5 月 12 日
(D) 5 月 19 日

解說 **看電子郵件和日期** （難易度）★

從電子郵件第一段第一句 I am contacting you to cancel my reservation for next week, May 12 to May 19.（這封信是為了取消我於下週 5 月 12 日至 19 日的預約。）可知，福頓先生原本預約了 5 月 12 日到 19 日的住宿，也就是說他從 5 月 12 日起開始休假，因此正確答案是 (C) May 12。也可以從渡假村寄來的確認信的 Arrival Date: May 12（抵達日：5 月 12 日）找到答案。

4. 福頓先生為什麼寄電子郵件給卡米爾莊園？

(A) 抱怨房間外的施工噪音
(B) 要求今年稍晚再多住一週
(C) 取消現有的渡假村預約
(D) 要求退回會員年費

解說 **看電子郵件；注意表示聯絡的關鍵句**
（難易度）★

從電子郵件第一段第一句 I am contacting you to cancel my reservation for next week, May 12 to May 19.（這封信是為了取消我於下週 5 月 12 日至 19 日的預約。）可知，寄這封郵件的目的是為了取消預約，因此正確答案是 (C) To cancel his existing reservation at the resort。

5. 關於福頓先生，文中暗示了什麼？

(A) 他的特殊要求將被應允。
(B) 他將被要求支付罰款。
(C) 他將收到另一個渡假村的預約。
(D) 他將可以移到另一個房間。

解說 兩篇文章型 **看信件（注意數字）；注意電子郵件開頭部分** （難易度）★★★

從信件的 Resort & Guest Information（渡假村及房客資訊）第一段第二句 Canceling this reservation less than 60 days prior to the check-in day will result in cancellation fees...（入住前 60 天內取消此預約將收取取消費……）可知，入住前 60 天內取消預約會收取費用。福頓先生取消訂房的電子郵件是 5 月 7 日送出，而他原本預約的是 5 月 12 日到 19 日的住宿，換言之他在入住前 60 天內取消，必須支付取消費，也可以理解成付罰款，因此正確答案是 (B) He will be required to pay a penalty.。

換句話說 正文 cancellation fees ➡ 選項 penalty

Day 10

本日主題

● 模擬測驗

Questions 1-2 refer to the following letter.

Interior Design
198 Madison Avenue
New York, NY 10016-4314

May 1

Julia Norton
324 Oak Tree Lane, Apartment 12
St. Paul, MN 55981

Dear Julia,

Having had the pleasure of mailing you *Interior Design* every month for the past three years, we are wondering if perhaps you haven't realized that your subscription ran out in March.

We mailed you our April issue and have not yet removed your name from our subscriber's list as we felt that you may have missed or misplaced our two previous renewal notices, one in January and one in February.

We have enclosed our renewal subscription card for you which provides for 12 issues of *Interior Design* at the low price of $1.50 per issue, or $1 less than the newsstand price of $2.50. As you can see, this represents a substantial savings over the course of a year.

We are looking forward to hearing from you soon and to the opportunity to provide you with another year's worth of insightful articles on how to make your home the most appealing that it can possibly be.

Sincerely yours,

Charles King

Charles King
Subscription Coordinator

1. Who is Julia Norton?

    (A) A house designer

    (B) A book editor

    (C) A magazine reader

    (D) A homeowner

2. What does the letter offer Ms. Norton?

    (A) A gift for her home

    (B) A discount in price

    (C) Free design newsletters

    (D) Automatic renewal

Questions 3-4 refer to the following message chain.

Peter Krushev   8:05 A.M.
I'm really late. There's been a crash on the expressway. My lanes are totally stopped.

Radha Murti   8:06 A.M.
Should I cancel our 8:30 staff meeting? Postpone it?

Peter Krushev   8:07 A.M.
Why not just change the agenda around? Move my report and my presentation to the end.

Radha Murti   8:09 A.M.
Good idea. I'll ask Mary to go over the budget proposal first. You've already reviewed it, right?

Peter Krushev   8:10 A.M.
Yeah. And after that, maybe everyone could discuss the team-building events scheduled for this fall. Come up with some new ideas.

Radha Murti   8:12 A.M.
Will do.

Peter Krushev   8:15 A.M.
Traffic has hardly budged, but I'm optimistic.

Radha Murti   8:16 A.M.
No hurry. We'll look forward to seeing you when you get here.

3. Why is the man delayed?

(A) He left his house late.
(B) His car broke down.
(C) The expressway is closed.
(D) There was an accident.

4. At 8:15 A.M., what does Peter Krushev most likely mean when he writes, "Traffic has hardly budged"?

(A) He has run out of gas.
(B) The traffic remains backed up.
(C) His car is running again.
(D) Traffic has been diverted.

RESIDENCES IN PARIS

Residence A. Two-story independent dwelling, located near the Luxembourg Garden, neighborhood park, and local schools. Living area of 265 square meters with large living room, dining room, kitchen, 4 bedrooms, and 2 bathrooms, and backyard. One-year lease.

Residence B. Executive apartment with approximately 120 square meters of living space, which consists of reception room for meetings, master suite, private office, and kitchen. Internet, telephone, and fax service provided. Monthly rental.

Residence C. Fifth floor apartment with stunning views over rooftops, with the Eiffel Tower in the foreground. The property is situated in a classic stone building and has 190 square meters of habitable area, which offers gallery entrance, dining room, kitchen, 3 bedrooms and a bathroom. Monthly or yearly rental.

Residence D. Superb newly constructed condominium on the 8th Arrondissement measuring 186 square meters with a combination of living room-dining room with fireplace, 2 bedrooms, single bathroom, and corner kitchen. No previous residents. In perfect condition with quality features and beautifully decorated. For purchase only.

D
A
Y
10

模擬測驗

5. What residence might be most appropriate for a business manager temporarily stationed in Paris?

(A) Residence A
(B) Residence B
(C) Residence C
(D) Residence D

6. What makes Residence D different from the other residences?

(A) It has a beautiful view.
(B) It has more bedrooms.
(C) It is for sale.
(D) It lacks a fireplace.

Questions 7-8 refer to the following e-mail.

TO: Rosalina Rodriguez <rrodriguez@mkrealty.com>

FROM: Patrick Chase <pchase@libsavings.com>

RE: A new stage in our relationship

DATE: September 20

Dear Ms. Rodriguez,

I want to thank you for giving me the opportunity to meet with you and members of your real estate staff to make our transition as smooth as possible.

I know that Brenda Williams, who was your personal banking assistant for many years, serviced your account with care and expertise and even made many friends at your firm. While her presence will be missed, I can promise that we will continue to offer you the fine service that she has always provided you.

Please contact me personally for any questions concerning your company's accounts or any requests related to financing, such as loans or lines of credit. My email address is listed above and my direct phone line is 777-3421.

The hospitality you showed me yesterday explains why Brenda held your realty firm in such high regard.

—Patrick

Patrick Thomas Chase
Liberty Savings and Loan

7. What is the main purpose of the e-mail?

(A) To market a new line of services
(B) To thank a client for a business dinner
(C) To continue a professional relationship
(D) To report the resignation of an employee

8. Who most likely is Patrick Chase?

(A) A realtor
(B) A banker
(C) A broker
(D) An accountant

Questions 9-11 refer to the following memo.

MEMO

To: Lisa Lee

From: Jeff Turner

Date: Wednesday 12/5

Time: 9:40

☐ VISITED

☑ TELEPHONED

☐ RETURNED YOUR CALL

☐ WILL CALL AGAIN

☐ PLEASE CALL

Message: He liked the produce that he ordered last week, especially our cabbage, onions, tomatoes, and cucumbers, because they are fresh and flavorful and good ingredients for the dishes at his café.
He is thinking of making weekly orders. So he would like you to send him an estimate for bulk buying by e-mail order. First, though, he wants to meet with you tomorrow morning to discuss the details.

Taken by: Jim Smith

9. Who is Jeff Turner?

   (A) A farmer
   (B) An office worker
   (C) A restaurant owner
   (D) A grocery store manager

10. What is Ms. Lee asked to do?

   (A) Make an estimate
   (B) Return a call
   (C) Delay an order
   (D) Inspect vegetables

11. When does Mr. Turner want to meet Ms. Lee?

   (A) On Tuesday
   (B) On Wednesday
   (C) On Thursday
   (D) On Friday

Your Microwave: Directions for Use

The microwave oven is now an essential part of most kitchens. During the summer or other hot times of the year, it's an excellent appliance to use because it won't heat up your kitchen the way a traditional gas or electric oven will.

A few words about using your microwave safely:

- The foods will be hot when removed from the oven, so it is best to use hot pads or wear insulated gloves.
- If the food is covered during cooking, make sure to leave a small portion vented or uncovered, so steam doesn't build up.
- Never use metal containers as microwaves bounce off their surfaces, which can cause a hazardous fire inside the oven.
- Don't heat water or other liquids beyond the time recommended by the maker or by the recipe. Superheating can occur even when plain water is heated in a clean cup for an excessive amount of time. The water will look normal, but when moved it can literally erupt out of the cup and cause burns.
- Refrain from operating the oven while it is empty. This can also cause overheating and start a fire, which is the appliance's biggest risk.
- Stand at least 3-4 feet away from the microwave when it is operating to avoid any exposure to microwaves.

NOTE: Never try to fix your own microwave. If it fails to work properly, always send it to an independent service center approved by our company.

12. According to the directions, what kind of cooking containers should be avoided?

(A) Plastic
(B) Ceramic
(C) Metal
(D) Porcelain

13. According to the directions, what should one do with a faulty microwave?

(A) Return it to the retail store
(B) Send it directly to the manufacturer
(C) Ship it to an approved repair facility
(D) Remove the broken control panel

14. Where would these directions most likely be found?

(A) In a manual
(B) In a warranty
(C) In a repair guide
(D) In a guaranty

D
A
Y
10

模
擬
測
驗

The Seattle Museum of Fine Art

With more than 500,000 visitors per year, the Seattle Museum of Fine Art is a wonderful destination for both residents and tourists. The museum houses a permanent collection of approximately 20,000 art pieces and 30,000 artifacts exhibited in an amazing 50,000 square meters of downtown gallery space.

Founded in 1895, the Seattle Museum of Fine Art is the oldest art museum in the Pacific Northwest. —[1]—. The five-story museum is internationally respected for its exquisite collections, special exhibitions, public lectures, and educational outreach programs.

The museum is continually changing as some pieces are loaned out to other museums, and especially as artworks from other collections are borrowed. —[2]—.

Among the many objects one can view in the museum's permanent collection are American paintings, European tapestries, Asian sculptures, and Native American handicrafts. —[3]—. In addition, the museum dedicates one gallery to temporary, visiting exhibitions of contemporary photography.

There is no admission fee. —[4]—. Suggested donations are:

$8 adults
$5 college students
$4 senior citizens
$3 school-age children

E-mail the museum curator at director@seattlemuseum.org to arrange for guided tours for groups from educational institutions.

15. What is true about the Seattle Museum of Fine Art compared to other Pacific Northwest museums?

(A) It is the largest in size.
(B) It has more artworks.
(C) It was established first.
(D) It has the most visitors.

16. What artwork is NOT mentioned as being part of the museum's permanent collection?

(A) Asian sculpture
(B) European tapestries
(C) Native American artifacts
(D) Contemporary photography

17. What group does the museum provide special services for?

(A) Visiting tourists
(B) Local artists
(C) Seattle residents
(D) School classes

18. In which of the following positions marked [1], [2], [3], and [4] does the following sentence best belong?
"This keeps the museum interesting, as there is something new to see on each visit."

(A) [1]
(B) [2]
(C) [3]
(D) [4]

MEMO

To: All Employees
From: Chief Information Officer, Hal Gold
Subject: The Simple Matter of Names and Addresses

Emma Simmons, head of the mailroom, has recently impressed upon me the need for a reminder regarding the correct handling of mail at our facility.

Any incoming mail should have the company name on it, in addition to the name of the personal recipient. Recently, we have had instances where the post office has, in its ongoing effort to decrease mis-deliveries, returned mail to the sender that was intended for us because it lacked a company name; this includes important invoices, statements and other materials. Please also consider the fact that all employees will someday resign or retire; after that time, any mail sent solely to them, even though intended for our company, may not be received. So please emphasize to your clients the importance of including our company name along with your own.

Furthermore, when preparing outgoing mail, kindly use our company envelopes for letters and our company labels for packages. These display our name so that if they cannot be delivered they will be returned to us. Incidentally, taping our company's self-sticking return address label to a package defeats the intended purpose of the adhesive on the back. Labels that are taped on can fall off and are more easily torn off, accidentally, by deliverers. This can also result in a package failing to be returned to us if it cannot be delivered.

Thank you as always for your cooperation and your commitment to effective communication.

19. What is the main topic of this memo?

(A) The company's new address
(B) The receipt of personal mail
(C) Company mail policy
(D) Improper packaging

20. The word "ongoing" in paragraph 2, line 3 is closest in meaning to

(A) latest
(B) continual
(C) intense
(D) random

21. According to the memo, what may happen if a mailing does not include the company name?

(A) It may be delivered only to the mailroom.
(B) It may be held until it is claimed.
(C) It may be returned to the sender.
(D) It may be treated as abandoned mail.

Asian Savers

—[1]—. Affluent Asians typically save nearly a quarter of their income, a survey released yesterday revealed. The report, issued by the private research foundation Global Economics, found that more than four in five top earners have preserved Northeast Asia's financial ethic, setting aside an average of one fourth of their earnings.

—[2]—. South Koreans stashed away 32 percent of their monthly income. They were followed by Chinese at 28 percent and the Taiwanese at 26 percent. Japanese came in a distant fourth at 16 percent.

—[3]—. Global Economics director Kwon Lee observed, "What we found is that higher-income earners surveyed across the Asia Pacific region save about a quarter of their income, which can enable them to take advantage of investment opportunities which further builds wealth."

—[4]—. Lee speculated that the long-term effects of such saving meant not only that individuals' net worth would rise, but also that more capital was available for investment in high-savings countries. This suggests that even low-income earners in a nation would benefit as job opportunities increased and salaries rose.

If you are interested in this position, please call me immediately at 341-8790 to arrange for an interview today or tomorrow. The job would start next Monday. We hope you might be interested in this unusual opportunity to expand your professional experience.

Thank you.

Patrick O'Brian
Recruitment Coordinator

30. Who is Ms. Gonzales?

(A) A newspaper reporter
(B) A personnel director
(C) An office manager
(D) A job applicant

31. What information is NOT requested on the form?

(A) Abilities
(B) Educational background
(C) Personal contact information
(D) Amount of previous experience

32. Why is Ms. Gonzales desirable for the position?

(A) Her filing skills
(B) Her publishing record
(C) Her current availability
(D) Her sales experience

33. What type of company is seeking an applicant?

(A) A department store
(B) A publisher
(C) A design company
(D) A law firm

34. According to the e-mail, why is a position open?

(A) A company is expanding its sales staff.
(B) A company is publishing a new book.
(C) A company is launching a new product line.
(D) A company is replacing an employee.

DAY
10

模擬測驗

Eileen De Souter
Rue du Marché-aux-Herbes 63
1000 Brussels

February 1

Credit Card Division
Euro Credit Union
Place de Brouckére 31-1000
Brussels-Belgium

Dear Euro Credit Officials:

I'm writing to you because my credit card is not working well.

Over the past one week, whenever a merchant or a restaurateur has tried to swipe my credit card so that I could make a payment, it has not worked. The clerks have then had to manually enter my card number into the card processor, and many do not even know how to do this. As I use my credit card for the vast majority of my daily purchases, this problem has become a major inconvenience for me.

Kindly send me a replacement card. I would be grateful if you would issue the new card with the same card number and the same expiration date as the original card: it is due to expire three years from now in August. Otherwise, I will need to contact each organization which keeps my card information on record for automatic payments (such as Internet retailers and local utilities) and change my card information.

At this time, I would also like to request that you raise my credit limit from 3,000 Euros to 5,000 Euros.

Thank you for your prompt assistance in these matters.

Sincerely yours,

Eileen De Souter

Eileen De Souter

Credit Card Division
Euro Credit Union
Place de Brouckére 31-1000
Brussels-Belgium

28 February

Ms. Eileen De Souter
Rue du Marché-aux-Herbes 63
1000 Brussels

Dear Ms. De Souter,

Enclosed please find your new EU card, which will not expire for a ten-year period. This card has the same credit card number as your prior card. We regret that you had trouble with your previous card, and we apologize for the delay in issuing you a new one.

I am happy to tell you that we have raised your monthly credit limit to the amount which you requested.

To activate your new card, please call 081-35-36-37 from your home phone. Please have both your card number and card expiration date ready to enter.

Afterwards, would you please cut your old card into several pieces and dispose of it securely? Please note that it will be invalid three weeks from the date of this letter.

Thank you for being a long-time customer of Euro Credit.

Very truly yours,

Gerald Pirotte

Gerald Pirotte
Customer Service Assistant
Credit Card Division

35. What is the main purpose of Ms. De Souter's letter?

(A) To terminate her credit card contract
(B) To request a larger cash advance
(C) To ask for an extension on a repayment
(D) To report a malfunctioning card

36. In the first letter, the word "prompt" in paragraph 5, line 1, is closest in meaning to

(A) stimulating
(B) kind
(C) timely
(D) helpful

37. How long did it take Euro Credit Union to respond to Ms. De Souter's letter?

(A) One week
(B) Two weeks
(C) Three weeks
(D) Four weeks

38. What does Euro Credit Union ask Ms. De Souter to do with her previous card?

(A) Return it to the company
(B) Store it securely
(C) Throw it away safely
(D) Retain it for her records

39. What request of Eileen De Souter does Euro Credit Union overlook?

(A) Her request for a higher credit limit
(B) Her request for the same card number
(C) Her request for a new replacement card
(D) Her request for the same card expiration date

PERSONNEL DIRECTORY: OMG GLOBAL FINANCE
Insurance Department

Carson, John: Commercial Real Estate (jcarson@omg.com)

Evans, Linda: Homeowners (levans@omg.com)

Gupta, Raj: Auto and Vehicles (rgupta@omg.com)

Hansen, Craig: Small Business (chansen@omg.com)

Johnson, Sally: Personal Liability (sjohnson@omg.com)

Lipinski, Peggy: Health and Medical (plipinski@omg.com)

Pushkin, Natasha: Life Insurance (npushkin@omg.com)

Sanchez, Pablo: Homeowners (psanchez@omg.com)

OMG GLOBAL FINANCE

TO: Members of the Insurance Department
FROM: Hugh Evans, Chief Operating Officer
RE: Office Restructuring
DATE: May 10

Thank you for your patience in awaiting your new office assignments. As you know, the firm's executives are dealing with major issues in some of our other divisions, particularly in corporate finance where profits are down, and in mortgage lending where new loans have slowed and staff is being reduced. Fortunately, your department is one of the most consistent performers in our group, and that is one of the reasons you are being assigned the redecorated offices in the newly renovated north wing.

Please use the information in the attached office index to identify your new location. I don't mean to be impersonal by not listing your individual names in the office index, but I want potential clients to communicate with the area, not the person. Also, we need to move you full-time staff members around from time to time within the department; making customers think that the person is equivalent to the coverage area creates misconceptions and causes miscommunication.

Thank you for your hard work. I hope you enjoy your improved office space.

OMG New Office Assignments: Insurance Department North Wing

Insurance Area	Office	Extension
Homeowners	NW-100	3210
Auto and Vehicles	NW-101	3211
Health and Medical	NW-102	3212
Personal Liability	NW-103	3213
Small Business	NW-104	3214
Commercial Real Estate	NW-105	3215
Life Insurance	NW-106	3216

40. Who would most likely process boat insurance?

    (A) Mr. Carson
    (B) Mr. Gupta
    (C) Ms. Johnson
    (D) Mr. Sanchez

41. In the memo, what does Mr. Evans say about the insurance department?

    (A) Its staff is being reduced.
    (B) Its profits are up.
    (C) Its performance is steady.
    (D) Its clients are increasing.

42. According to the memo, why are offices being re-assigned?

    (A) Due to an expansion in staffing
    (B) Due to the construction of a new building
    (C) Due to a change in employee assignments
    (D) Due to renovation of current office space

43. In what office will Peggy Lipinski work?

    (A) NW-100
    (B) NW-101
    (C) NW-102
    (D) NW-103

44. What is Sally Johnson's telephone extension?

    (A) 3212
    (B) 3213
    (C) 3214
    (D) 3215

模擬測驗

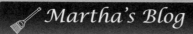 *Martha's Blog*

"A Clean Home is a Happy Home"

Many of my Web site readers have asked me to sum up my cleaning principles and philosophy. So for them, I offer this post today.

Principle 1 [timing]: Sooner rather than later

Spills and stains on household items are much easier to clean up when you attack them right away. If you wait until the next day, they may never come out. Tablecloth, curtain, and carpet stains are easiest to remove when they're fresh. The longer you wait, the more chance the stain has to set.

Principle 2 [location]: From the top down

Working from high to low almost always works better in cleaning situations. When you're cleaning the entire house, start on the top floor and work your way down to avoid tracking through rooms you have already cleaned. Likewise, when you're cleaning a room, first dust the ceiling fan and light fixtures, followed by window frames and wall hangings. Moving downward, clean the furniture, baseboards, and then floors. This ensures that any dust shaken loose from on high does not settle on something you've already cleaned below.

Principle 3 [kind of cleanings]: Clean dry, then wet

When you're cleaning a room, start with dry methods (dusting, sweeping, and vacuuming), then move on to wet methods (glass cleaning and mopping). This way, there will be less dirt floating around in the room to cling to wet surfaces.

Principle 4 [cautious cleaning]: First do no harm

Use your gentlest cleaning methods first and move up to more aggressive techniques only if necessary. Better to put up with a small spot on your stovetop, for instance, than to ruin the surface by scraping it with steel wool.

Martha encourages feedback from readers. Type in your comment below. She'll do her best to respond.

COMMENT

As a stay-at-home dad with two boys aged 7 and 9, I consider myself something of a cleaning expert, and I read your blog and generally follow your advice. For example, "From top down" is really important also when cleaning windows and mirrors. Starting up high and working your way down saves a lot of time and energy because one's motions follow gravity, and it's easier to clean in a downward motion.

I do want to point out, however, that there is a big exception to your "Sooner rather than later principle." Mud tracked onto a carpet is far easier to clean when you've let it dry first. In fact, if you let it dry overnight and become crumbly, you can just vacuum it up. Attacking it with a wet cloth almost guarantees a stain.

By the way, Martha, I wish I had read this week's blog last week. I probably wouldn't have used bleach on my shirt to get rid of a coffee stain. Now there's a big white spot that's almost as bad as the original stain.

Chuck Fitzgerald

MARTHA'S RESPONSE

Chuck, sorry to hear about that shirt! But experience is one of the best teachers and I think nearly all of us have to have a bad experience with bleach before we realize how *not* to use it. You make a really important point about carpet cleaning. Thanks for sharing it with our readers. In fact, I should have included "mud" under "Clean dry rather than wet when possible." This principle holds true not only for carpets but also sometimes for clothes, too, when mud or dry substances such as caked dirt are involved. Thank you for your insight!

45. According to the blog, what room should be cleaned first?

(A) An upstairs bedroom
(B) A downstairs closet
(C) A first floor living room
(D) A furnished basement

46. According to the blog, what type of cleaning should be done first?

(A) Floor mopping
(B) Mirror cleaning
(C) Rug vacuuming
(D) Window washing

47. What cleaning principle does Mr. Fitzgerald disagree with?

(A) Principle 1
(B) Principle 2
(C) Principle 3
(D) Principle 4

48. What is true about Mr. Fitzgerald?

(A) He runs a cleaning company.
(B) He owns a laundry service.
(C) He does not work outside his house.
(D) He manages his own apartment building.

49. What does Martha indicate about the cleaning of clothes?

(A) It is best to avoid strong detergents.
(B) Bleach is often an effective cleaner.
(C) Sometimes it is best to let a stain dry.
(D) Sooner is always better than later.

TO:	Kathleen Polanski <kpolanski@ctmail.com>
FROM:	Ananda Jeyraj <ajeyraj@ctmail.com >
SUB:	scheduling interviews
DATE:	July 3rd

Kathleen,

We've gotten a lot of response to the want ad that we posted on our Web site for a receptionist. I've gone through the 15 résumés and selected the top 10 candidates. Could you contact them and arrange for interviews and skills tests (mainly keyboarding checks)? Let's try to hold all of the interviews from July 14th-15th, preferably one after another in the afternoon (that's more efficient). The applicants can take the skills tests as soon as their interviews are over.

I'm really tied up with important issues like negotiating a new employee insurance plan and initiating our paid holiday and sick-leave policies, so I'd like you to take care of the personnel stuff. Of course, we'll do the 30-minute interviews together, like usual, in the conference room. Please be sure to enter the times of the interviews into my office schedule when they're decided so I know when to be available.

Thanks.

Ananda
Director
Human Resources

Personal Schedule, Jeyraj, Human Resources

July 14	July 15
9:00 Meeting with CFO	9:00 Meeting with insurance agents
9:30 〃 〃	9:30 〃 〃
10:00 Sick leave work	10:00 Strategic planning meeting
10:30 〃 〃	10:30 〃 〃
11:00 Budget meeting	11:00 〃 〃

11:30 " "	11:30 Prepare a planning report
12:00-1:00 Lunch	12:00-1:00 Lunch
1:00 HR staff meeting	1:00
1:30 Interview preparation (receptionist)	1:30 Interview preparation (receptionist)
2:00 [possible interview]	2:00 [possible interview]
2:30 Kristen Rackas	2:30 Clara Harrington
3:00 Carl Stephanoplous	3:00 Ricardo Rodriquez
3:30 Audrey Shiller	3:30 Elaine Johnson
4:00 Discussion of candidates	4:00 Discussion of candidates
4:30 [possible interview]	4:30 Final decision on hiring

TO:	Ananda Jeyraj <ajeyraj@ctmail.com>
FROM:	Kathleen Polanski <kpolanski@ctmail.com>
SUB:	Re: scheduling interviews
DATE:	July 4th

Dear Ananda,

I contacted the candidates you selected. A few withdrew their applications, but I have scheduled all of the rest for interviews, except for one who *will* interview but we haven't yet decided on her time slot. As you probably noticed, I have already updated your schedule. Unfortunately, the conference room is unavailable (the sales department has reserved it for a two-day seminar), but I'll find another appropriate place and let you know.

Good luck with your other work, especially the new sick-leave policy; the old one is not very popular.

Kathleen
Recruitment Coordinator
Human Resources

50. What is the main purpose of the first e-mail?

(A) To assign a task
(B) To post a want ad
(C) To announce a new policy
(D) To re-schedule an appointment

51. What is NOT true of Mr. Jeyraj's present duties?

(A) He is working on a staff insurance package.
(B) He is implementing a new vacation policy.
(C) He is scheduling interviews for job applicants.
(D) He is reforming the company's medical leave rules.

52. How many candidates will likely be interviewed?

(A) Seven
(B) Nine
(C) Ten
(D) Fifteen

53. What can be inferred about Ms. Polanski and Mr. Jeyraj?

(A) They are applying for the same position.
(B) They are colleagues in the personnel department.
(C) They plan to attend the same conference.
(D) They have the same job title.

54. What part of the interview process needs to be determined?

(A) The length of the interviews
(B) The candidates to interview
(C) The venue of the interviews
(D) The dates for the interviews

D
A
Y
10

模擬測驗

中譯 問題 1-2：請看以下信件。 →原文請見 p. 178

室內設計
紐約 NY10016-4314
麥迪遜大道 198 號

5 月 1 日

[1]茉莉亞・諾頓
聖保羅 MN 55981
橡樹巷 324 號 12 號公寓

親愛的茉莉亞：

很榮幸過去這三年每個月都能寄給您《室內設計》雜誌，不過我們在想，[1]您或許不曉得您的訂閱已於三月到期。

[1]我們已將四月號寄給您，也尚未將您從我們的訂閱者名單中移除，因為我們認為您可能是錯過或遺失了我們前兩次的續訂通知，一次在一月，一次在二月。

[2]隨信附上續訂卡，提供 12 期《室內設計》每期 1.50 美元的優惠價，也就是較定價 2.5 美元低 1 美元。如您所見，這表示一年內您可以省下相當可觀的金額。

我們期待盡快收到您的消息，並期望有機會再為您提供一整年有價值又富洞察力的文章，告訴您如何讓府上變得更吸引人。

訂閱專員
查爾斯・金恩
查爾斯・金恩

敬上

單字

□ run out 到期
□ remove 動 移除
□ misplace 動 記不起來把…放在何處
□ represent 動 意味著，表示

□ substantial 形 大量的
□ insightful 形 具有洞察力的
□ appealing 形 魅力十足的

1. 誰是茉莉亞・諾頓？
   (A) 房屋設計師
   (B) 書籍編輯
   (C) 雜誌讀者
   (D) 房屋所有人

█解說█ **找出收件人**   （難易度）★★

從信件的格式可知，這封信的收件人是茉莉亞・諾頓。而從第一段的 you haven't realized that your subscription ran out in March（您或許不曉得您的訂閱已於三月到期）與第二段的 We mailed you our April issue and have not yet removed your name from our subscriber's list...（我們已將四月號寄給您，也尚未將您從我們的訂閱者名單中移除……）可推知，收件人茉莉亞・諾頓是雜誌讀者，因此正確答案是 (C) A magazine reader。

█換句話說█ █正文█ subscription, subscriber ➡ █選項█ reader

2. 這封信提供諾頓小姐什麼東西？
   (A) 給她家的禮物
   (B) 價格折扣
   (C) 免費設計通訊
   (D) 自動更新

█解說█ **注意數字；在鼓勵續訂的題目中，正確答案通常是折扣或贈品** （難易度）★★

從第三段第一句 We have enclosed our renewal subscription card for you which provides for 12 issues of *Interior Design* at the low price of $1.50 per issue, or $1 less than the newsstand price of $2.50.（隨信附上續訂卡，提供 12 期《室內設計》每期 1.50 美元的優惠價，也就是較定價 2.5 美元低 1 美元。）可知，提供比定價更低的價格，也就是價格折扣，因此正確答案是 (B) A discount in price。

█換句話說█ █正文█ at the low price of $1.50 per issue, or $1 less than the newsstand price of $2.50 ➡ █選項█ A discount in price

DAY
10

模擬測驗

彼得‧克魯雪夫　　　　　　　　　　　　　　　　　　　早上 8:05
我真的要遲到了。³高速公路上發生車禍，我這個車道完全不動了。

雷得哈‧墨提　　　　　　　　　　　　　　　　　　　　早上 8:06
要取消我們 8 點 30 分的員工會議嗎？還是延期？

彼得‧克魯雪夫　　　　　　　　　　　　　　　　　　　早上 8:07
何不改一下議程就好？把我的報告和發表移到最後。

雷得哈‧墨提　　　　　　　　　　　　　　　　　　　　早上 8:09
好主意。我會請瑪麗先說一下預算提案。你已經看過了，對吧？

彼得‧克魯雪夫　　　　　　　　　　　　　　　　　　　早上 8:10
對。在那之後，或許大家可以討論一下預定今年秋天舉辦的團隊打造活動，想一些新的點
子。

雷得哈‧墨提　　　　　　　　　　　　　　　　　　　　早上 8:12
好的。

彼得‧克魯雪夫　　　　　　　　　　　　　　　　　　　早上 8:15
⁴車子還是一動也不動，但我保持樂觀。

雷得哈‧墨提　　　　　　　　　　　　　　　　　　　　早上 8:16
不急，我們期待看到你的到來。

單字

□ crash 名 相撞事故　　　　　　　□ agenda 名 議程
□ expressway 名 高速公路　　　　　□ budge 動 稍微移動
□ postpone 動 延後　　　　　　　　□ optimistic 形 樂觀的

3. 男子為什麼被耽擱了？
(A) 他太晚出門了。
(B) 他的車故障了。
(C) 高速公路關閉了。
(D) 有場意外。

解說 可從題目裡的主詞的訊息推測出正確
答案
（難易度）★★

題目的 man 指的是彼得‧克魯雪夫，他在一開始
的訊息中提到自己要遲到了，接著解釋說是因為
There's been a crash on the expressway.（高速
公路上發生車禍。）也就是發生意外，因此正確答
案是 (D) There was an accident.。

換句話說 **正文** crash ➡ **選項** accident

---

4. 早上 8 點 15 分時，彼得‧克魯雪
夫寫「車子還是一動也不動」最有
可能是什麼意思？
(A) 他已經沒有油了。
(B) 交通還在堵塞。
(C) 他的車又能跑了。
(D) 交通已經紓解。

解說 從前後文判斷特定語句的意思
（難易度）★★

在這句話之後，彼得‧克魯雪夫接著說 but I'm
optimistic（但我保持樂觀），用表示轉折的 but 來
連接，可知前面提到的情況不太理想。雷得哈‧墨
提接著對他說 No hurry.（不急。）可推知動彈不
得的狀況持續著，彼得‧克魯雪夫還在路上，因
此正確答案是 (B) The traffic remains backed up.。

中譯 問題 5-6：請看以下廣告。

巴黎的住宅

住宅 A：兩層樓獨立住宅，靠近盧森堡花園、社區公園及當地的學校。居住面積為 265 平方公尺，有大客廳、餐廳、廚房、四間臥室、兩間浴室及後院。租約一年。

住宅 B：⁵商務公寓，居住面積近 120 平方公尺，包含會議接待室、主臥室、私人辦公室及廚房。提供網路、電話及傳真服務。按月租賃。

住宅 C：五樓公寓，屋頂有絕佳景致，前方就是艾菲爾鐵塔。這間住宅位於一古典石造建築內，居住面積有 190 平方公尺，包含長廊入口、餐廳、廚房、三間臥室和一間浴室。按月或按年租賃。

住宅 D：華麗的新建公寓大樓，位於第八區，面積為 186 平方公尺，有附壁爐的起居室兼餐廳、兩間臥室、一間浴室及角落廚房。未曾有房客入住，屋況完美，有高品質外觀及美麗的裝潢。⁶只賣不租。

單字

- □ dwelling 名 住宅
- □ master suite 主臥室
- □ stunning 形 驚人的
- □ rooftop 名 屋頂
- □ foreground 名 前景
- □ superb 形 華麗的
- □ condominium 名 大廈式公寓
- □ arrondissement 名（巴黎的行政區）區

5. 哪一個住宅最適合短期派駐巴黎的
   商業經理人？
   (A) 住宅 A
   (B) 住宅 B
   (C) 住宅 C
   (D) 住宅 D

解說 由關鍵字判斷　　　難易度 ★★

從住宅 B 的 executive apartment（商務公寓）、reception room for meetings（會議接待室）和 private office（私人辦公室）等關鍵字可知，這是專為商務人士設計的住宅。另外，從最後的 monthly rental（按月租賃）可知適合短期租賃，因此正確答案是 (B) Residence B。

6. 住宅 D 和其他住宅有什麼不同？
   (A) 有美麗的景觀。
   (B) 有更多臥室。
   (C) 打算出售。
   (D) 缺少壁爐。

解說 多款產品拿出來比較時，通常在相同位置會列出一樣的項目；注意有 only 的句子　　難易度 ★★

住宅 A 到 D 的屋況說明最後分別寫著租賃條件，住宅 A 是 one-year lease（租約一年），住宅 B 是 monthly rental（按月租賃），住宅 C 是 monthly or yearly rental（按月或按年租賃），住宅 D 則是 for purchase only（只賣不租），換言之，只有住宅 D 僅供出售，因此正確答案是 (C) It is for sale.。

換句話說　正文 for purchase ➡ 選項 for sale

D
A
Y
10

模擬測驗

213

中譯 問題 7-8：請看以下電子郵件。

收件人：蘿莎莉娜・羅德里格斯 <rrodriguez@mkrealty.com>
寄件人：派崔克・崔斯 <pchase@libsavings.com>
[7]回覆：我們關係的新階段
日期：9 月 20 日

親愛的羅德里格斯小姐：

我想謝謝您給我這個機會，讓我跟您以及您房地產公司的員工見面，以盡可能順利地完成轉交。

我知道[8]您多年來的個人理財助理布蘭達・威廉斯一直小心、專業地管理您的帳戶，更在您的公司內交了許多朋友。[7]雖然她即將離開，但我能保證我們會一如既往地繼續為您提供良好的服務。

[8]若您對貴公司的帳戶有任何問題，或對理財有任何需求，例如貸款或信貸額度，請直接與我聯絡。我的電子郵件帳號如上，專線電話是 777-3421。

您昨日的熱情款待說明了為何布蘭達對您的房地產公司有這麼高的評價。

派崔克

派崔克・湯瑪斯・崔斯
[8]自由儲貸

單字

- □ transition 名 交接，轉交
- □ smooth 形 順利的
- □ expertise 名 專業
- □ presence 名 在場，出席

- □ financing 名 財務，融資
- □ line of credit 信用額度
- □ hospitality 名 殷勤招待，好客
- □ hold ... in high regard 給予…高度評價

7. 這封電子郵件的主要目的為何？
(A) 行銷新的服務
(B) 感謝客戶的商業晚餐
(C) 維持專業關係
(D) 報告一名員工離職

解說 從 RE 判斷目的　　難易度 ★★

從 RE: A new stage in our relationship（回覆：我們關係的新階段），以及第二段最後一句 While her presence will be missed, I can promise that we will continue to offer you the fine service...（雖然她即將離開，但我能保證我們會繼續為您提供良好的服務……）可知，這封信的目的是要維持雙方的專業關係，因此正確答案是 (C) To continue a professional relationship。

---

8. 派崔克·崔斯最有可能是誰？
(A) 地產商
(B) 銀行員
(C) 經紀人
(D) 會計師

解說 從 From 判斷寄件人；從關鍵字推測職業　　難易度 ★★

從第二段可知，寄件人派崔克·崔斯與布蘭達·威廉斯任職於同一家公司。從第二段第一句的 Brenda Williams, who was your personal banking assistant for many years（您多年來的個人理財助理布蘭達·威廉斯）可知，布蘭達在銀行工作，因此正確答案是 (B) A banker。從第三段第一句的 financing（理財）、loans（貸款）、lines of credit（信貸額度），以及最後署名處下面的公司名稱 Liberty Savings and Loan（自由儲貸）也可知道派崔克·崔斯是銀行員。

備忘便條

¹⁰收件人：李麗莎　　　　　　¹¹日期：12 月 5 日星期三
⁹留言人：傑夫・透納　　　　　時間：9:40

☐ 拜訪　　　　　　　　　　☑ 來電
☐ 回電　　　　　　　　　　☐ 會再來電
☐ 請致電

留言內容：他喜歡上週訂的農產品，尤其是我們的高麗菜、洋蔥、番茄和小黃瓜，因為新鮮又可口，⁹很適合做為他咖啡店的餐點的食材。
他考慮要每週訂購，¹⁰所以他想請你將透過電子郵件大量訂購的估價單寄給他。但首先，¹¹他想明天早上和你碰面討論細節。

記錄者：吉姆・史密斯

單字
☐ produce 名 農產品
☐ flavorful 形 美味的
☐ ingredient 名 原料，材料
☐ estimate 名 估價單
☐ bulk buying 大量購買

9. 傑夫‧透納是誰？

(A) 農夫

(B) 辦公室員工

(C) 餐廳主人

(D) 雜貨店經理

解說　從便條的 From 判斷留言者

難易度　★★

從 From（留言人）可知來電者是傑夫‧透納，便條記錄的是他的留言內容。從第一句的 because they are fresh and flavorful and good ingredients for the dishes at his café（因為新鮮又可口，很適合做為他咖啡店的餐點的食材）可知，傑夫‧透納是咖啡店的老闆，也就是餐廳主人，因此正確答案是 (C) A restaurant owner。

換句話說　正文 café ➡ 選項 restaurant

10. 李小姐被要求做什麼？

(A) 製作估價單

(B) 回電

(C) 延遲訂單

(D) 檢查蔬菜

解說　從便條的 To 判斷收件人；注意表示要求的關鍵句

難易度　★★

從 To（收件人）可知，這是給李麗莎的留言。留言內容第二段有一表示要求的關鍵句 So he would like you to send him an estimate...（所以他想請你將估價單寄給他……），可知是要求李麗莎提供估價單，也就是要她製作估價單，因此正確答案是 (A) Make an estimate。

11. 透納先生想要什麼時候和李小姐碰面？

(A) 週二

(B) 週三

(C) 週四

(D) 週五

解說　從 Date 判斷日期；注意最後一句

難易度　★★

從 Date（日期）可知，留言日期是 12 月 5 日星期三。留言內容寫道 he wants to meet with you tomorrow morning（他想明天早上和你碰面），可知透納先生想要在週四碰面，因此正確答案是 (C) On Thursday。

DAY 10

模擬測驗

中譯 問題 12-14：請看以下資訊。 →原文請見 p. 184

您的微波爐：**14 使用說明**

微波爐現在是許多廚房不可或缺的一部分，在夏天或一年之中其他炎熱的時節，它是絕佳的設備，因為它不會像傳統瓦斯爐或電子爐般，使廚房溫度升高。

14 關於安全使用微波爐的方法，有下列幾點：

◆ 食物移出微波爐時溫度很高，所以最好使用隔熱墊或穿戴隔熱手套。

◆ 如果食物加熱時有加蓋，請記得開一個小孔，或稍微移開蓋子，這樣蒸氣才不會在裡面累積。

◆ **12 千萬不要使用金屬容器**，因為微波會從金屬的表面反射，這可能會導致微波爐內起火，發生危險。

◆ 水或其他液體的加熱時間不可超過標示或食譜建議的時間。就算白開水放在乾淨的杯子中，也可能因加熱時間過長導致過熱。水看起來雖然是正常的，但只要移動杯子就可能會噴出，導致燙傷。

◆ 避免微波爐空轉，這也可能導致過度加熱而起火，這是此設備最大的風險。

◆ 微波爐運轉時，請離微波爐至少三到四英尺遠，避免暴露於微波下。

注意：千萬別試圖自己修理微波爐。**13 如果微波爐無法正常運作，請送到本公司認可的獨立服務中心。**

單字

□ essential 形 必要的	□ hazardous 形 危險的
□ appliance 名 設備	□ superheat 動 過度加熱
□ insulated glove 隔熱手套	□ excessive 形 過度的，過多的
□ vent 動 給…開孔	□ erupt 動 噴出
□ steam 名 蒸氣	□ refrain from... 避免…
□ bounce off... 從…反射回去	□ exposure 名 暴露

12. 根據使用說明的內容，應避免使用哪一種烹調容器？
    (A) 塑膠
    (B) 陶器
    (C) 金屬
    (D) 瓷器

解說　注意內含 Never、Don't 的句子　　難易度 ★★

使用說明內列出了幾點注意事項，其中第三點寫 Never use metal containers...（千萬不要使用金屬容器……），可知應避免使用金屬容器，因此正確答案是 (C) Metal。

---

13. 根據使用說明的內容，微波爐故障時該怎麼辦？
    (A) 拿回零售店
    (B) 直接寄給製造商
    (C) 送到經認可的維修中心
    (D) 移除故障的控制盤

解說　注意 NOTE　　難易度 ★★

從最後 NOTE 的第二句 If it fails to work properly, always send it to an independent service center approved by our company.（如果微波爐無法正常運作，請送到本公司認可的獨立服務中心。）可知，故障時應送到經認可的維修中心修理，因此正確答案是 (C) Ship it to an approved repair facility。

換句話說　正文 send ➡ 選項 Ship
　　　　　正文 service center ➡ 選項 repair facility

---

14. 這些使用說明最有可能出現在哪裡？
    (A) 在使用手冊中
    (B) 在保證書中
    (C) 在維修指引中
    (D) 在保證書中

解說　注意標題與粗體字　　難易度 ★★

標題寫著 Directions for Use（使用說明），也就是說這是使用說明書，因此正確答案是 (A) In a manual。有時候使用手冊上不會寫出 Directions for Use 之類的標題，這時可以從注意事項的 A few words about using your microwave safely:（關於安全使用微波爐的方法，有下列幾點：），或是條列的內容中推測出正確答案。

換句話說　正文 Directions for Use ➡ 選項 manual

DAY 10

模擬測驗

西雅圖美術館

西雅圖美術館每年有超過 50 萬名遊客來訪，不論對當地居民或觀光客而言都是非常棒的景點。美術館的永久收藏品有近兩萬件藝術品和三萬件工藝品，在市中心驚人的五萬平方公尺藝廊空間中展出。

¹⁵西雅圖美術館成立於 1895 年，是美國西北部歷史最悠久的藝術博物館。—[1]—。這棟五層樓高的美術館因其精緻的館藏、特展、公開講座及教育推廣服務而享譽國際。

¹⁸美術館本身也不斷變化中，除了因為某些館藏會出借給其他美術館，更因為也從其他美術館借來館藏藝術品。—[2]—。

¹⁶大家可以看到的美術館永久收藏品包括美國繪畫、歐洲掛毯、亞洲雕塑和美國原住民手工藝品。—[3]—。此外，美術館還將其中一個藝廊用做當代攝影作品的特設展展場。

無須入場費。—[4]—。建議捐款金額如下：

成人　　　　8 美元
大學生　　　5 美元
年長者　　　4 美元
學齡兒童　　3 美元

¹⁷若想為教育機關安排團體導覽，請寄電子郵件給美術館館長。電子郵件信箱是 director@seattlemuseum.org。

單字

□ house 動 收藏，藏有　　　　　□ sculpture 名 雕塑
□ permanent 形 永久的　　　　　□ handicraft 名 手工藝品
□ artifact 名 工藝品　　　　　　□ dedicate 動 奉獻，獻出
□ exquisite 形 精緻的　　　　　　□ contemporary 形 當代的
□ outreach 名 延伸，推廣　　　　□ admission fee 入場費
□ tapestry 名 掛毯　　　　　　　□ curator 名 館長

15. 關於西雅圖美術館和其他美國西北部的博物館之比較，何者為真？
(A) 它的規模是最大的。
(B) 它的藝術品比較多。
(C) 它是第一個成立的。
(D) 它有最多的遊客。

解說 注意各段落開頭的内容　難易度 ★★

從第二段第一句的 the Seattle Museum of Fine Art is the oldest art museum in the Pacific Northwest（西雅圖美術館是美國西北部歷史最悠久的藝術博物館）可知，西雅圖美術館是該地區第一個成立的藝術博物館，因此正確答案是 (C) It was established first.。

換句話說　正文 is the oldest art museum ➡ 選項 was established first

16. 美術館的永久收藏品中沒有提到哪一種藝術作品？
(A) 亞洲雕塑
(B) 歐洲掛毯
(C) 美洲原住民工藝品
(D) 當代攝影作品

解說 NOT 問句通常可用消去法解題

難易度 ★★

第四段第一句提到美術館的永久收藏品，包括 American paintings（美國繪畫）、European tapestries（歐洲掛毯）、Asian sculptures（亞洲雕塑）、Native American handicrafts（美國原住民手工藝品），並沒有攝影作品，因此正確答案是 (D) Contemporary photography。當代攝影作品是特設展非常設展，不屬於永久收藏品。

17. 美術館對哪一種團體提供特別服務？
(A) 來參觀的觀光客
(B) 當地藝術家
(C) 西雅圖居民
(D) 學校班級

解說 注意最後一句　難易度 ★★

從廣告的最後一句 E-mail the museum curator at ... to arrange for guided tours for groups from educational institutions.（若想為教育機關安排團體導覽，請寄電子郵件給美術館館長。）可知，美術館提供服務的對象是教育機關，也就是學校班級，因此正確答案是 (D) School classes。

換句話說　正文 groups from educational institutions ➡ 選項 School classes

18. 下列句子最適合放在 [1]、[2]、[3]、[4] 哪一個位置？
「如此能讓美術館常保新鮮、有趣，因為每次參觀都有新的展品可以看。」
(A) [1]
(B) [2]
(C) [3]
(D) [4]

解說 讀懂插入句的意思，找出主詞 This 所指的内容　難易度 ★★

從插入句的「每次參觀都有新的展品可以看」可推知，美術館的展品並非一成不變。而第三段提到因為出借館藏及借入展品，美術館本身也不斷變化中，跟插入句互為呼應，因此放在第三段最後最適合，正確答案是 (B) [2]。插入句的主詞 This 指的是前一句話全部的内容。

DAY
10

模擬測驗

中譯 問題 19-21：請看以下備忘便條。

備忘便條

收件人：所有員工
寄件人：首席資訊長 海爾・高德
主旨：關於姓名和住址的二三事

收發室主管艾瑪・西蒙斯最近讓我強烈意識到，¹⁹需要提醒大家如何正確處理我們公司的信件。

任何來信上面除了收件人姓名之外，都應該要有公司名。最近，²⁰因郵局持續努力減少誤投，²¹將原本要寄給我們但未寫上公司名的信件退回給寄件人，其中包括重要的請款單、報表和其他資料。請各位也要考量到一點，不管哪一個員工總有一天會辭職或退休，在那之後，就算原本是要寄給公司的信件，如果只寫了那些收件人的名字，也不會寄達。因此，請向你的客戶強調同時寫上我們的公司名及你自己姓名的重要性。

另外，準備外寄郵件時，懇請使用我們公司的信封，以及有我們公司標誌的包裹，因為上有公司名，若是無法投遞，便會退回我們公司。附帶一提，在包裹上黏貼公司的自黏回郵地址標籤，背面的黏著劑可能失效，黏在上面的標籤可能會脫落，也非常容易被遞送人員意外扯掉，這也可能導致無法投遞時，難以退回包裹。

謝謝各位總是配合公司政策，並願意進行有效的溝通。

單字

- impress on... 使…（人）牢記在心
- reminder 名 提醒
- incoming mail 寄來的郵件
- recipient 名 接受者
- intend for... 指定給…
- invoice 名 請款單
- solely 副 僅僅
- outgoing mail 寄出的郵件
- incidentally 副 順道一提
- adhesive 名 黏著劑
- tear off... 撕下…，扯掉…
- commitment 名 承諾

19. 這份備忘便條的主題是什麼？
(A) 公司的新地址
(B) 個人郵件的接收
(C) 公司郵件處理方針
(D) 不適當的包裝

解說 **注意開頭內容**　　難易度 ★★

從第一段的 the need for a reminder regarding the correct handling of mail at our facility（需要提醒大家如何正確處理我們公司的信件）可知，這是關於公司郵件處理方式的便條，因此正確答案是 (C) Company mail policy。在企業內部公告的文章中，經常出現正確答案是 company policy 的題目。

換句話說　正文 facility ➡ 選項 company

20. 第二段第三行的單字 ongoing，最接近哪一個意思？
(A) 最近的
(B) 繼續的
(C) 強烈的
(D) 隨機的

解說 **從前後文推測意思**　　難易度 ★★

the post office has, in its ongoing effort to decrease mis-deliveries...（因郵局持續努力減少誤投……）的 ongoing 是「持續的，不間斷的」的意思，選項中最接近的是 (B) continual，為正確答案。

21. 根據備忘便條的內容，如果郵件未寫公司名，可能會發生什麼事？
(A) 可能只會寄到收發室。
(B) 可能被扣留，直到有人領回為止。
(C) 可能會退回給寄件人。
(D) 可能被當成廢棄郵件處理。

解說 **找出 company name**　　難易度 ★★

從第二段第二句的 the post office has ... returned mail to the sender that was intended for us because it lacked a company name（郵局……將原本要寄給我們但未寫上公司名的信件退回給寄件人）可知，沒有寫上公司名的話，郵件可能會被退回給寄件人，因此正確答案是 (C) It may be returned to the sender.。

DAY
10

模擬測驗

中譯 問題 22-25：請看以下文章。 →原文請見 p. 190

亞洲儲蓄者

—[1]—。一項昨天發布的調查顯示，²³富裕的亞洲人通常會存下近四分之一的收入。²²這份報告是由私人研究基金會全球經濟所發布，報告中發現五個高收入者中有超過四人保有東北亞的金錢道德觀，平均存下四分之一的收入。

—[2]—。²⁵南韓人每月存下收入的 32%。接著是中國人的 28% 和台灣人的 26%，日本人差距較遠，排名第四，為 16%。

—[3]—。全球經濟的董事李權評論道：「我們發現，所調查的亞太區高收入者大約會存下收入的四分之一，這讓他們能善加利用投資機會，為他們累積更多財富。」

—[4]—。李推測，這種儲蓄的長期影響不只代表個人的資產淨值會增加，同時，²⁴在這些高存款國家也會有更多資本可供投資。這表示，就算是該國的低收入者也會因工作機會增加和薪資上漲而受益。

單字

□ affluent 形 富裕的	□ set aside... 儲存…
□ typically 副 典型地	□ earnings 名 所得
□ quarter 名 四分之一	□ stash away... 儲存…
□ income 名 收入	□ speculate 動 推測
□ preserve 動 保有，維持	□ capital 名 資本
□ ethic 名 倫理標準，道德準則	

22. 根據文章內容，誰發布了這份關於存款的報告？
(A) 政府機構
(B) 研究機構
(C) 私人企業
(D) 公立基金會

解說 正確答案是組織名稱時，選項裡通常會換個方式表達 （難易度）★

從第一段第二句 The report, issued by the private research foundation Global Economics...（這份報告是由私人研究基金會全球經濟所發布……）可知，報告是由一研究機構所發布，因此正確答案是 (B) A research institute。

換句話說 **正文** research foundation ➡ **選項** research institute

---

23. 根據文章內容，這份調查指出什麼？
(A) 有錢的亞洲人會存下收入的 25%。
(B) 日本人通常存得比其他亞洲人多。
(C) 台灣人的收入最高。
(D) 南韓人傾向不存錢。

解說 注意開頭內容 （難易度）★★

從第一段第一句的 Affluent Asians typically save nearly a quarter of their income...（富裕的亞洲人通常會存下近四分之一的收入……）可知，有錢的亞洲人會存下收入的四分之一，因此正確答案是 (A) Wealthy Asians set aside 25 percent of their earnings。

換句話說 **正文** save ➡ **選項** set aside
正文 a quarter of ➡ **選項** 25 percent
正文 income ➡ **選項** earnings

---

24. 關於高存款率的國家，李權暗示了什麼？
(A) 他們應增加消費。
(B) 他們過度依賴出口。
(C) 他們強調教育的重要性。
(D) 他們的經濟成長狀況良好。

解說 注意最後一段 （難易度）★★

第四段的 Lee speculated ... that more capital was available for investment in high-savings countries.（李推測……在這些高存款國家也會有更多資本可供投資。）提到，高存款國家有更多資本可供投資，可推測其經濟能夠成長，因此正確答案是 (D) They have good conditions for economic growth。

---

25. 下列句子最適合放在 [1]、[2]、[3]、[4] 哪一個位置？
「南韓人是最節儉的。」
(A) [1]
(B) [2]
(C) [3]
(D) [4]

解說 注意插入句的前後文 （難易度）★★

第二段依存款比例高低舉出四個高存款國家，其中韓國排名第一。把插入句放在第二段一開始最適合，因為緊接著便舉出具體的數字 South Koreans stashed away 32 percent of their monthly income.（南韓人每月存下收入的 32%。）因此正確答案是 (B) [2]。

DAY 10

模擬測驗

中譯 問題 26-29：請看以下線上對話。

早川智夫　早上 10:24
所有人都該看看二樓穿戴式設備的展示，尤其是 [28]智慧型手錶和健康監控設備。[26]我們應該要擺一些在店裡賣！

茱莉·瑞伊　早上 10:26
我接下來會去。我現在正在看備份儲存系統，還有外接硬碟等。[27]不過沒什麼新意。

馬克·強森　早上 10:27
整體來說是個不錯的展售會。好幾家公司都有展示自家剛上市的智慧型手機，在五樓的攤位，我們應該要進一些來賣！

索菲亞·弗朗西斯卡　早上 10:30
有人要去聽 11 點開始的系統安全演講嗎？我們可能會想向客戶推薦其中的一些服務。

肯·克蘭施米特　早上 10:40
我沒有時間，我在看下一代 [28]高畫質電視。

索菲亞·弗朗西斯卡　早上 10:45
[29]我們真的需要交換一下意見。

馬克·強森　早上 10:45
對，我也覺得這很重要，[29]這有助於我們決定訂單。

索菲亞·弗朗西斯卡　早上 10:46
中午到一樓的皇家咖啡館如何？

早川智夫　早上 10:47
好，聽起來不錯。

單字
- □ wearable 名
  可穿戴在身上的物品（常用複數形）
- □ fitness 名 健康
- □ carry 動 備有（商品）
- □ innovation 名 創新
- □ booth 名 貨攤
- □ inventory 名 存貨
- □ definition 名 解析度

26. 參與對話的人可能在哪一種公司
工作？
(A) 電子零售商
(B) 貿易公司
(C) 批發店
(D) 會議中心

解說 可從關鍵字或關鍵句推測公司類型

難易度 ★★

從對話中的 smart watches（智慧型手錶）、fitness monitors（健康監控設備）、smartphones（智慧型手機）、high definition TVs（高畫質電視）等關鍵字可知，對話者在電子產品相關公司工作。從早川智夫早上 10 點 24 分的訊息 We've got to carry some of these in our store!（我們應該要擺一些在店裡賣！）可知是零售店，因此正確答案是 (A) An electronics retailer。

---

27. 關於儲存設備，瑞伊小姐提到了
什麼？
(A) 它們變得愈來愈吸引人。
(B) 它們比以前更節省成本。
(C) 它們最近沒什麼改變。
(D) 它們比以前種類更多。

解說 找出與 storage device 同義的單字

難易度 ★★

茱莉・瑞伊在早上 10 點 26 分的訊息中提到 I'm looking at back-up storage systems...（我正在看備份儲存系統……）back-up storage systems 就是題目中的 storage devices。接著她馬上評論 Not much innovation here, though.（不過沒什麼新意。）也就是說沒有什麼改變，因此正確答案是 (C) They have recently changed very little.。

---

28. 對話中沒有提到哪一種設備？
(A) 健康追蹤器
(B) 電腦化的手錶
(C) 筆記型電腦
(D) 電視

解說 NOT 問句通常可用消去法解題

難易度 ★★

對話中提到了 fitness monitors（健康監控設備）、smart watches（智慧型手錶）、high definition TVs（高畫質電視），分別與 (A)、(B)、(D) 相符。沒有提到筆電，因此正確答案是 (C) Laptops。

DAY
10

---

29. 早上 10 點 45 分時，弗朗西斯卡
小姐寫「我們真的需要交換一下
意見」最有可能是什麼意思？
(A) 她想交換觀點。
(B) 她想檢查她的筆記。
(C) 她想比較價格。
(D) 她想確認購買的東西。

解說 從前後文判斷特定語句的意思

難易度 ★★★

compare notes 是「交換意見」的意思，就算不知道意思，也可以從接下來馬克・強森的訊息 It'll help us decide our orders.（這有助於我們決定訂單。）推知，交換意見有助於下訂單，因此正確答案是 (A) She wants to exchange viewpoints.。

換句話說　正文 compare notes ➡ 選項 exchange viewpoints

模擬測驗

30 求職申請書
派遣員工股份有限公司
招募辦公室

30 姓名：愛蓮娜‧岡薩雷斯　　　　　　　　31 電話：080-555-1218

31 地址：新南威爾斯 2310 布萊頓
　　　　康拉德大道 #5 438 號

31 電子郵件：elenagonzales@instmail.com

應徵職位：辦公室助理

31 專長領域：歸檔、打字、電話銷售、試算表管理

相關經驗年資：六

32 何時可上班：可立即上班。週一到週五早上 8 點到晚上 7 點都可以，週六也可以工作。

你如何得知這個職缺？
《布萊頓日報》徵人版

收件人：elenagonzales@instmail.com
寄件人：temporaryofficestaff@uninet.com
回覆：你最近的應徵及可能的面試

親愛的岡薩雷斯小姐：

這封信是想詢問你能否填補我們某個客戶公司的緊急職缺，33 是一家本地的出版社。34 設計部其中一名員工，是編輯助理，因為健康因素突然離職。

這個職位的工作包含書籍版面編排，以及準備出版用的完稿。

如果你對這個職位有興趣，請立即打電話給我，安排今天或明天面試，電話是 341-8790。工作將於下週一開始。希望你對這個特別的機會感興趣，擴展你的專業經驗。

謝謝你。

招募負責人
派崔克‧歐布萊恩

單字

□ urgent 形 緊急的　　　　　　　　│　□ abruptly 副 突然地

30. 岡薩雷斯小姐是誰？
(A) 新聞記者
(B) 人事主任
(C) 辦公室經理
(D) 工作應徵者

解說 看表單，從 Name 判斷求職者

(難易度) ★

從表單標題可知是求職申請書，上面的 Name: Elena Gonzales（姓名：愛蓮娜·岡薩雷斯）則是求職者姓名，因此正確答案是 (D) A job applicant。

---

31. 表單中沒有要求填寫哪一項資訊？
(A) 能力
(B) 教育背景
(C) 個人聯絡資料
(D) 過去經驗多寡

解說 確認表單上各個項目

(難易度) ★

選項內容可替換成表單上各項目，必須逐一對照。表單上的 Skill areas（專長領域）、Phone, Address, E-mail（電話、地址、電子郵件）、Years of related experience（相關經驗年資）分別與 (A)、(C)、(D) 相符。表單上沒有要求填寫教育背景，因此正確答案是 (B) Educational background。

---

32. 為什麼岡薩雷斯小姐是這個職位的適合人選？
(A) 她的歸檔技巧
(B) 她的出版紀錄
(C) 她最近可以上班
(D) 她的銷售經驗

解說 兩篇文章型 注意電子郵件開頭的內容；判斷表單上各個項目

(難易度) ★★

從電子郵件第一段第一句的 urgent opening（緊急職缺）可知，此公司現在非常缺人，而從表單的 Availability: Can start immediately.（何時可上班：可立即上班。）可知，岡薩雷斯小姐隨時可上班，因此正確答案是 (C) Her current availability。

---

33. 哪一種公司正在徵人？
(A) 百貨公司
(B) 出版社
(C) 設計公司
(D) 律師事務所

解說 注意電子郵件開頭的內容

(難易度) ★

從電子郵件第一段第一句的 an urgent opening at one of our client firms, a local publishing company（我們某個客戶公司的緊急職缺，是一家本地的出版社）可知，正在徵人的是一家出版社，因此正確答案是 (B) A publisher。

換句話說 正文 publishing company ➡ 選項 publisher

---

34. 根據電子郵件的內容，為什麼會有這個職缺？
(A) 公司正擴大招募業務員。
(B) 公司正要出版新書。
(C) 公司正要發表新的生產線。
(D) 公司正要替換一名員工。

解說 看電子郵件

(難易度) ★★

從電子郵件第一段第二句的 One of the staff members ... has had to abruptly leave due to medical reasons.（其中一名員工……因為健康因素突然離職。）可知，有一名員工離職，所以需要遞補員工，因此正確答案是 (D) A company is replacing an employee。

中譯 問題 35-39：請看以下信件。

³⁵艾琳・德・蘇特
布魯塞爾 1000
藥草市場街 63 號

³⁷2 月 1 日

歐元信用合作社
信用卡部門
比利時 布魯塞爾
德布克廣場 31-1000

親愛的歐元信用合作社員工：

³⁵我寫這封信是因為我的信用卡無法正常使用。

過去一個禮拜以來，我無論是在商店或餐廳消費，刷卡付款都無法成功，後來店員必須在卡片處理機上手動輸入我的卡號，其中有許多人甚至不知道該怎麼做。由於我每天的購物大多使用信用卡，這個問題已經對我造成嚴重的不便。

懇請寄給我一張替換的信用卡。³⁹如果你能寄發一張和原卡相同卡號和到期日的卡片，我會很感激：原卡將在三年後的八月到期。不然的話，我還得聯絡每一個持有我卡片資訊、用以進行自動扣款的商家（例如網路零售商和地方公用事業公司），並更改我的卡片資訊。

同時，我也想要求調高信用額度，從 3000 歐元調為 5000 歐元。

非常感謝你對這些事的³⁶及時協助。

艾琳・德・蘇特
艾琳・德・蘇特
敬上

單字
- □ merchant 名 商人
- □ restaurateur 名 餐館老闆
- □ swipe 動 刷（卡）
- □ manually 副 手動地
- □ vast 形 大量的
- □ utility 名
  公用事業（電力、自來水等）公司
- □ prompt 形 迅速的，及時的

歐元信用合作社
信用卡部門
比利時 布魯塞爾
德布克廣場 31-1000

³⁷2 月 28 日

艾琳・德・蘇特小姐
布魯塞爾 1000
藥草市場街 63 號

親愛的德・蘇特小姐：

隨信附上您新的歐元信用卡，³⁹使用期限為 10 年。這張卡片的卡號和之前的卡片一樣。對於前一張卡片造成的問題我們感到遺憾，也為延誤寄發新卡一事致歉。

很高興告訴您，我們已經調高您每個月的信用額度，達到您要求的金額。

請以家用電話致電 081-35-36-37，以啓用新卡。請同時準備好卡號及卡片到期日，以便輸入。

³⁸之後，可否請您將舊卡剪斷，並安全地丟棄它？請注意，舊卡將於這封信所標註的日期的三週後失效。

感謝您長久以來對歐元信用的支持。

信用卡部門
客服助理
吉拉德・皮羅特
吉拉德・皮羅特

敬上

單字

□ activate 動 開卡　　　　　　　　| □ dispose of... 丟棄…

35. 德·蘇特小姐信件的主要目的為何？
- (A) 終止她的信用卡契約
- (B) 要求更高額的預借現金
- (C) 要求延期償還
- (D) 通報故障的信用卡

解說 注意書信的版面格式和表示原因的關鍵句
(難易度) ★

從第一封信最上方和左下角的署名可知，寄件人是德·蘇特小姐。信件一開頭提到 I'm writing to you because my credit card is not working well.（我寫這封信是因為我的信用卡無法正常使用。）可知目的是告知信用卡有問題，因此正確答案是 (D) To report a malfunctioning card。

換句話說 正文 not working well ➡ 選項 malfunctioning

---

36. 在第一封信中，第五段第一行的單字 prompt，最接近哪一個意思？
- (A) 刺激的
- (B) 仁慈的
- (C) 及時的
- (D) 有益的

解說 從前後文推測意思
(難易度) ★★

信中的 prompt assistance 是「及時協助」的意思。prompt 有「及時的，迅速的」之意，同樣表示「及時的」之意的 (C) timely 是正確答案。其他的同義字還有 quick、immediate 等。

---

37. 歐元信用合作社花了多久時間回覆德·蘇特小姐的信？
- (A) 一週
- (B) 兩週
- (C) 三週
- (D) 四週

解說 兩篇文章型 找出兩封信的日期；注意信頭
(難易度) ★★

第一封要求重新核發信用卡的信中，信頭的日期寫著 February 1（2 月 1 日），第二封發卡通知信的日期則寫著 28 February（2 月 28 日），可見信用卡公司花了約一個月，也就是四週的時間才回信，因此正確答案是 (D) Four weeks。

---

38. 歐元信用合作社要德·蘇特小姐如何處理舊卡？
- (A) 寄回給公司
- (B) 安全地存放
- (C) 安全地丟棄
- (D) 保留做為紀錄之用

解說 注意第二封信中表示要求的關鍵句
(難易度) ★★

從第二封信第四段第一句的 Afterwards, would you please cut your old card into several pieces and dispose of it securely?（之後，可否請您將舊卡剪斷，並安全地丟棄它？）可知，信用卡公司要她安全地丟棄舊卡，因此正確答案是 (C) Throw it away safely。

換句話說 正文 dispose of it ➡ 選項 Throw it away
正文 securely ➡ 選項 safely

39. 歐元信用合作社忽略了艾琳‧德‧蘇特的哪一項要求？

(A) 她要求更高的信用額度

(B) 她要求同樣的卡號

(C) 她要求新的替換卡片

(D) 她要求同樣的卡片到期日

解說　兩篇文章型　注意數字　難易度　★★★

從第一封信第三段第二句的 the same expiration date as the original card: it is due to expire three years from now in August（和原卡相同到期日：原卡將在三年後的八月到期）可知，艾琳‧德‧蘇特要求的是三年後的八月到期的信用卡。但從第二封信第一段第一句的 which will not expire for a ten-year period（使用期限為 10 年）可知，新卡的有效期限為 10 年，和原要求不符，因此正確答案是 (D) Her request for the same card expiration date。

人員名錄：OMG 全球金融

保險部

約翰・卡爾森：商業地產 (jcarson@omg.com)

琳達・伊凡斯：房屋所有人 (levans@omg.com)

40 拉吉・古普塔：汽車與交通工具 (rgupta@omg.com)

克拉格・韓森：小型企業 (chansen@omg.com)

44 莎莉・強森：個人責任 (sjohnson@omg.com)

43 佩吉・李賓斯基：健康與醫療 (plipinski@omg.com)

娜塔莎・普希金：人壽保險 (npushkin@omg.com)

帕布羅・桑切斯：房屋所有人 (psanchez@omg.com)

單字

□ commercial 形 商業的

□ homeowner 名 自有住宅的所有者

□ personal liability　個人責任

OMG 全球金融

收件人：保險部員工

寄件人：首席營運長　修・伊凡斯

回覆：辦公室調整

日期：5 月 10 日

謝謝各位耐心等待新的辦公室分配。各位也知道，公司高層正在處理其他部門的重大問題，特別是企業融資部門，最近盈利下降了，還有抵押貸款部門也因新貸款減少，裁減了部分員工。還好，41 你們部門在我們團隊中表現很穩定，因此 42 你們將被分配到重新裝潢、位於翻修過的北翼的辦公室。

請利用附件的辦公室索引資訊，找出你新的位置。沒有在辦公室索引中列出各位的姓名，並不是故意要顯得沒有人情味，而是我希望潛在客戶能與該部門溝通，而非特定個人。同時，我們需要偶爾讓各位，也就是全職員工在部門中輪調；讓客戶以為某個人代表某個保險範圍會造成誤解，導致溝通不佳。

謝謝你們的辛勤工作，希望你們喜歡改良後的辦公空間。

□ mortgage 名 抵押
□ consistent 形 一致的
□ impersonal 形 冷淡的，不近人情的

□ be equivalent to... 等同於…
□ misconception 名 誤解
□ miscommunication 名 溝通不良

OMG 新辦公室分配：北翼保險部

保險範圍	辦公室	分機
房屋所有人	NW-100	3210
汽車與交通工具	NW-101	3211
[43]健康與醫療	NW-102	3212
[44]個人責任	NW-103	3213
小型企業	NW-104	3214
商業地產	NW-105	3215
人壽保險	NW-106	3216

40. 誰最有可能處理船隻保險？
(A) 卡爾森先生
(B) 古普塔先生
(C) 強森小姐
(D) 桑切斯先生

解說 **對照名錄的人名與所屬單位** 難易度 ★

船隻是交通工具，因此是由負責 Auto and Vehicles（汽車與交通工具）的拉吉・古普塔處理，正確答案是 (B) Mr. Gupta。

---

41. 在備忘便條中，關於保險部伊凡斯先生說了什麼？
(A) 員工裁減中。
(B) 利潤提高了。
(C) 表現很穩定。
(D) 客戶增加中。

解說 **看備忘便條；從 From 判斷寄件人** 難易度 ★★★

從備忘便條的 From（寄件人）與 To（收件人）可知，這是修・伊凡斯給保險部員工的便條。從第一段第三句的 your department is one of the most consistent performers in our group（你們部門在我們團隊中表現很穩定）可知，保險部表現穩定，因此正確答案是 (C) Its performance is steady.。

換句話說 正文 consistent ➡ 選項 steady

---

42. 根據備忘便條的內容，辦公室為什麼要重新分配？
(A) 因為員工數增加了
(B) 因為蓋了新大樓
(C) 因為員工任務改變
(D) 因為現有的辦公空間翻修

解說 **看備忘便條；注意各段落最後一句** 難易度 ★★★

從備忘便條第一段第三句最後的 you are being assigned the redecorated offices in the newly renovated north wing（你們將被分配到重新裝潢、位於翻修過的北翼的辦公室）可知，因為辦公室翻修所以重新分配，因此正確答案是 (D) Due to renovation of current office space。

---

43. 佩吉・李賓斯基會在哪一個辦公室工作？
(A) NW-100
(B) NW-101
(C) NW-102
(D) NW-103

解說 兩篇文章型 **對照名錄和辦公室索引** 難易度 ★★★

從名錄可知，佩吉・李賓斯基負責的是 Health and Medical（健康與醫療），而根據新辦公索引，承辦健康與醫療業務的辦公室在 NW-102，因此正確答案是 (C) NW-102。

---

44. 莎莉・強森的電話分機是幾號？
(A) 3212
(B) 3213
(C) 3214
(D) 3215

解說 兩篇文章型 **對照名錄和辦公室索引** 難易度 ★★★

從名錄可知，莎莉・強森負責的是 Personal Liability（個人責任），而根據新辦公索引，承辦個人責任業務的辦公室是 NW-103，分機號碼為 3213，因此正確答案是 (B) 3213。

中譯 問題 45-49：請看以下部落格文章、意見和回應。

瑪莎的部落格

「乾淨的家就是快樂的家」

許多網站上的讀者要我總結我的打掃原則和哲學，所以為了他們，今天貼出這篇文章。

[47] 原則 1〔時機〕：早點比晚點好
潑濺在家具上的液體或汙漬馬上處理，會比較容易清乾淨。如果等到隔天才處理，可能永遠都洗不掉了。桌巾、窗簾、地毯的汙漬在剛沾到的時候最容易清除。放得愈久，汙漬愈有可能附著其上。

原則 2〔位置〕：從上到下
[45] 打掃時，從上到下的效果總是比較好。當你打掃整棟房屋時，先從最高樓層開始，一路向下，避免踏過你已經掃好的房間。同理，當你打掃某個房間時，先清理天花板的風扇和燈具的灰塵，接著是窗框和牆壁吊飾，然後繼續往下打掃家具、踢腳板，然後是地板。這樣能確保高處掃落的灰塵不會落在下方已經打掃好的地方。

原則 3〔打掃方式〕：先乾後濕
[46] 當你打掃房間時，先從乾的方法開始（拂塵、掃灰、吸塵），然後換濕的方法（擦玻璃和拖地）。如此一來，就不會有太多灰塵飄浮在房間裡，黏附在潮濕的表面上。

原則 4〔小心打掃〕：首重不損壞
先使用最溫和的清潔方法，只在必要的時候，才換比較激進的方法。舉例來說，如果爐子上有個小汙點，最好容忍它的存在，而不是用鋼刷刮傷爐子表面。

瑪莎鼓勵讀者的回饋。請在下方打上你的意見，她會盡可能回應。

DAY
10

模擬測驗

單字

- □ sum up... 總結…
- □ spill 名 溢出的東西
- □ stain 名 汙漬
- □ light fixture 燈具
- □ baseboard 名 踢腳板
- □ vacuum 動 用吸塵器吸
- □ float around 飄浮
- □ cling to... 黏附於…
- □ gentle 形 溫和的
- □ aggressive 形 激進的
- □ put up with... 忍耐…
- □ scrape 動 刮，擦

意見

[48]身為一個全職父親，有七歲和九歲的兒子，我覺得自己算得上是個清潔專家。我拜讀了你的部落格，並大致上遵循你的建議。舉例來說，擦窗戶和擦鏡子時，「從上到下」原則也非常重要。從高處開始，一路往下，能省下很多時間和精力，因為人的動作是順著重力的，向下的清理動作會比較簡單。

[47]但是，我想指出一點，那就是你的「早點比晚點好」原則有一個很大的例外。沾到地毯上的泥巴如果先等它乾，會更容易清理。事實上，如果你讓它乾燥一個晚上，等它變脆，之後只要把它吸起來就好。如果用濕布去清它，幾乎注定會留下汙漬。

另外，瑪莎，我真希望自己上週就讀到這週的部落格文章，這樣我或許就不會用漂白水去清潔襯衫上的咖啡漬。現在襯衫上有個白點，幾乎和原來的汙漬一樣糟糕。

查克‧費茲傑羅

單字

□ motion 名 動作　　　　　　　　　□ overnight 副 一整晚
□ gravity 名 重力，地心引力　　　　□ crumbly 形 易碎的
□ track 動 留下痕跡　　　　　　　　□ bleach 名 漂白劑

瑪莎的回應

查克，襯衫的事我很遺憾！但經驗是最好的老師，我認為幾乎所有人都得先有過漂白水的慘痛經驗，才會知道如何「不」使用它。地毯清潔的事，你說了非常重要的一點，謝謝你和我們的讀者分享。事實上，我應該把「泥巴」列入「[49]盡可能乾的時候清而不是濕的時候」原則，這個原則不只適用於地毯，有時候也可以用在衣物沾到泥巴或是結塊的泥土之類乾的物質時。謝謝你的洞見！

單字

□ hold true for... 適用於…　　　　　□ insight 名 洞見
□ caked 形 結塊的

---

45. 根據部落格的內容，應該先清理哪一個房間？
(A) 樓上的臥房
(B) 樓下的衣櫃
(C) 一樓的客廳
(D) 有家具的地下室

解說 **看部落格文章；注意各段落開頭內容**
難易度 ★★

部落格文章提到四個打掃的大原則，從原則 2 第一句 Working from high to low almost always works better in cleaning situations.（打掃時，從上到下的效果總是比較好。）可知，應從高處開始打掃，因此正確答案是 (A) An upstairs bedroom。

---

46. 根據部落格的內容，應該先做哪一類的清潔？
(A) 拖地
(B) 擦鏡子
(C) 吸地毯
(D) 洗窗戶

解說 **看部落格文章；注意各段落開頭內容**
難易度 ★★

從原則 3 第一句的 When you're cleaning a room, start with dry methods (dusting, sweeping, and vacuuming)...（當你打掃房間時，先從乾的方法開始〔拂塵、掃灰、吸塵〕……）可知，應該從吸地之類的乾式清潔做起，因此正確答案是 (C) Rug vacuuming。

---

47. 費茲傑羅先生不同意哪一個清潔原則？
(A) 原則 1
(B) 原則 2
(C) 原則 3
(D) 原則 4

解說 兩篇文章型 **看意見和部落格文章；注意各段落開頭內容**
難易度 ★★

從意見的第二段第一句 I do want to point out, however, that there is a big exception to your "Sooner rather than later principle."（但是，我想指出一點，那就是你的「早點比晚點好」原則有一個很大的例外。）可知，他不同意「早點比晚點好」的打掃原則，也就是原則 1，因此正確答案是 (A) Principle 1。

---

48. 關於費茲傑羅先生的敘述，何者為真？
(A) 他經營一家清潔公司。
(B) 他擁有一家洗衣公司。
(C) 他沒有在外面工作。
(D) 他管理自己的公寓大樓。

解說 **注意意見開頭的內容**
難易度 ★★

從意見第一句的 As a stay-at-home dad（身為一個全職父親）可知，費茲傑羅先生是全職的家庭主夫，沒有在外面工作，因此正確答案是 (C) He does not work outside his house.。

換句話說 正文 stay-at-home ➡ 選項 does not work outside his house

49. 關於衣服的清潔，瑪莎提出什麼看法？

(A) 最好不要使用強力清潔劑。

(B) 漂白水通常是有效的清潔劑。

(C) 有時候最好讓汙漬自己變乾。

(D) 早點總比晚點好。

解說 找出回應中提到 clothes 的部分

(難易度) ★★★

瑪莎的回應倒數第二句寫道 This principle holds true not only for carpets but also sometimes for clothes... （這個原則不只適用於地毯，有時候也可以用在衣物……），這裡的 principle 指的就是前面的 Clean dry rather than wet when possible（盡可能乾的時候清而不是濕的時候），也就是說讓汙漬變乾之後再清比較好，因此正確答案是 (C) Sometimes it is best to let a stain dry.。

收件人：凱瑟琳・波蘭斯基 <kpolanski@ctmail.com>
寄件人：阿南達・傑拉吉 <ajeyraj@ctmail.com>
主旨：安排面試
日期：7 月 3 日

凱瑟琳：

我們張貼在網站上徵求接待員的徵人廣告收到很多回應，我已經看過 15 份收到的履歷表，選出了前 10 名應徵者。**50 你能不能和他們聯絡，並安排面試和技能測試**（主要是確認打字能力）**？** 我們試著在 7 月 14 到 15 日舉行所有面試，最好排在下午，一個接一個（這樣比較有效率）。應徵者可以在面試後馬上接受技能測試。

51 我現在忙著處理像是協商新的員工保險計畫、啓動有薪假和病假政策等重要議題，所以我希望你處理這項人事問題。當然，我們會像往常一樣，一起在會議室裡進行 30 分鐘的面試。面試安排好之後，記得要在我的辦公行事曆中輸入面試時間表，我才知道我什麼時間要空下來。

謝謝。

53 人力資源部
主任
阿南達

單字

□ go through... 仔細看過…
□ preferably 副 最好，更好地
□ initiate 動 開始

□ paid holiday 有薪假
□ sick-leave 名 病假

個人行事曆，傑拉吉，人力資源部

7 月 14 日	7 月 15 日
9:00 和 CFO 開會	9:00 和保險代理人開會
9:30　〃　　〃	9:30　〃　　〃
10:00 關於病假的工作	10:00 策略計畫會議
10:30　〃　　〃	10:30　〃　　〃
11:00 預算會議	11:00　〃　　〃
11:30　〃　　〃	11:30 準備計畫報告

12:00-1:00 午餐	12:00-1:00 午餐
1:00 人資員工會議	1:00
1:30 面試準備（接待員）	1:30 面試準備（接待員）
2:00 〔可能的面試〕	2:00 〔可能的面試〕
2:30 克莉絲汀‧瑞卡斯	2:30 克萊拉‧哈靈頓
3:00 卡爾‧史帝芬諾普洛斯	3:00 里卡多‧羅德里格斯
3:30 奧黛莉‧席勒	3:30 伊蓮‧強森
4:00 討論應徵者	4:00 討論應徵者
4:30 〔可能的面試〕	4:30 聘用人選最終討論

收件人：阿南達‧傑拉吉 <ajeyraj@ctmail.com>
寄件人：凱瑟琳‧波蘭斯基 <kpolanski@ctmail.com>
主旨：回覆：安排面試
日期：7 月 4 日

親愛的阿南達：

我聯絡了你選出的應徵者，有幾個人取消了應徵，但[52]其他人的面試我都已經安排好了，除了有一個會來面試，但我們還沒有決定她的時段。你可能注意到了，我已經更新了你的行事曆。[54]不巧的是，會議室無法使用（業務部已經先預約，要舉辦為期兩天的講座），但我會找另一個合適的空間，到時再告訴你。

祝你其他的工作好運，特別是新的病假政策，舊有政策實在不是很受歡迎。

[53]人力資源部
招募專員
凱瑟琳

┌───┐
│ **單字**   │
│ □ withdraw 動 收回，取消   │ □ time slot 時段 │
└───┘

50. 第一封電子郵件的主要目的為何？
    (A) 指派任務
    (B) 張貼徵人廣告
    (C) 宣布新的政策
    (D) 重新安排行程

解說 看第一封電子郵件；注意表示要求的關鍵句 難易度 ★★

從第一封電子郵件可知，人資部主任已經看過應徵者的履歷，並挑出適合人選，他接著說 Could you contact them and arrange for interviews and skills tests?（你能不能和他們聯絡，並安排面試和技能測試？）可知是要部下安排面試時間，也就是指派任務，因此正確答案是 (A) To assign a task。

51. 關於傑拉吉先生現有工作的描述，何者為非？
    (A) 他正在處理員工保險方案。
    (B) 他正要實施新的休假政策。
    (C) 他正要為工作應徵者安排面試。
    (D) 他正要改革公司的病假規則。

解說 看第一封電子郵件；NOT 問句通常可用消去法解題 難易度 ★★

從第一封電子郵件第二段第一句可知，傑拉吉先生正忙於 negotiating a new employee insurance plan（協商新的員工保險計畫）、initiating our paid holiday and sick-leave policies（啟動有薪假和病假政策）等工作，分別和選項 (A)、(B)、(D) 相符，因此正確答案是 (C) He is scheduling interviews for job applicants.。

52. 可能會有幾個應徵者接受面試？
    (A) 七個
    (B) 九個
    (C) 十個
    (D) 十五個

解說 兩篇文章型 看行事曆與第二封電子郵件；注意數字 難易度 ★★★

數一數行事曆上的人名，可知有六個人將參加面試。第二封電子郵件提到 I have scheduled all of the rest for interviews, except for one who will interview but we haven't yet decided on her time slot（其他人的面試我都已經安排好了，除了有一個會來面試，但我們還沒有決定她的時段），換言之總共有七個人會參加面試，因此正確答案是 (A) Seven。

DAY. 10

模擬測驗

53. 關於波蘭斯基小姐和傑拉吉先生，可以做出哪一項推論？
(A) 他們應徵同一個職位。
(B) 他們是人事部門的同事。
(C) 他們計畫參加同一場會議。
(D) 他們有同樣的職稱。

解說 兩篇文章型 注意兩封電子郵件的版面格式 （難易度）★★★

兩封電子郵件最後的署名都寫有寄件人、所屬單位與職稱，可知兩人都在 Human Resources（人力資源部）工作，換言之，兩人是人事部門的同事，因此正確答案是 (B) They are colleagues in the personnel department.。

換句話說 正文 Human Resources ➡ 選項 personnel

---

54. 面試過程的哪一個部分需要決定？
(A) 面試的長度
(B) 參加面試的應徵者
(C) 面試的場地
(D) 面試的日期

解說 找出與面試過程有關的敘述 （難易度）★★★

第二封電子郵件第一段的最後提到 Unfortunately, the conference room is unavailable, but I'll find another appropriate place and let you know.（不巧的是，會議室無法使用，但我會找另一個合適的空間，到時再告訴你。）也就是說面試的場地有待決定，因此正確答案是 (C) The venue of the interviews。

換句話說 正文 place ➡ 選項 venue

● 重要字彙一覽表

以下整理常出現在 Part 7 的字彙。標示 類 者為意思相近或相關的字彙。

組織‧部門

□ division	名（公司等的）處，課，部門	
□ department	名（公司等的）部，部門	
□ personnel	名 人事部	類 human resources, H.R.
□ accounting	名 會計	
□ public relations	名 公關	
□ facility	名 設施，設備	類 factory, school, hospital
□ corporation	名 公司	類 firm, enterprise, company
□ headquarters	名 總部	類 head office
□ branch	名 分公司，分店	

職稱‧職務

□ president	名 總經理	類 executive, CEO
□ vice president	名 副總經理	類 executive
□ auditor	名 稽核員	
□ branch manager	名 分店經理	
□ manager	名 經理	類 supervisor
□ employer	名 雇主	
□ employee	名 員工	類 staff member, associate
□ accountant	名 會計師	
□ office clerk	名 職員，事務員	
□ receptionist	名 櫃台人員，接待員	
□ trainee	名 還在試用期的員工	

徵才廣告

□ applicant	名 應徵者	類 candidate
□ work experience	名 工作經驗	類 employment history, professional career
□ qualification	名 資格條件	
□ requirement	名 必備條件	
□ salary	名 薪水	類 payment, remuneration, compensation
□ position	名 職位，職務	類 occupation
□ management	名 管理	類 administration
□ recommendation letter	名 推薦信	類 reference
□ résumé	名 履歷表	類 curriculum vitae, C.V.
□ immediate	形 直屬的	類 direct
□ leave	名 休假	
□ submit	動 提出	類 send in, turn in

報價單・繳款通知單

□ specification	名 明細	
□ balance	名 餘款	類 amount due
□ estimate	名 估價單	類 quotation
□ terms	名 條款	類 conditions
□ charge	名 費用 動 收費	
□ bill	名 帳單	類 invoice
□ customized	形 客製的	類 individualized, tailored, bespoke
□ fixed	形 固定的	類 flat

訂貨

□ order	動 訂貨	類 place an order for...
□ ship	動 出貨	類 send, dispatch
□ shipment	名 貨物	
□ shipping date	名 出貨日	
□ reminder	名 催款信	類 collection letter
□ delivery	名 送貨	
□ in stock	有庫存	
□ out of stock	無庫存	

買賣・交易

□ contract	名 契約	類 agreement
□ warranty	名 保證書	類 form of guarantee
□ distributor	名 經銷商	類 sales agency
□ shipping fee	名 運費	類 charge for delivery
□ free of charge	免費	類 for free, complimentary
□ defect	名 瑕疵	類 fault
□ refund	動 退費	類 repay, reimburse
□ purchaser	名 購買者	類 buyer
□ retailer	名 零售商	類 retail store
□ wholesaler	名 批發商	類 wholesale dealer

協商．交涉

□ negotiate	動 協商	類 bargain, make a deal
□ suggestion	名 提議	類 recommendation, proposal
□ solution	名 解決方法	類 answer
□ compromise	動 妥協	類 meet halfway
□ concession	名 讓步	
□ confrontation	名 對決	類 showdown, conflict
□ coordinator	名 協調者	類 organizer
□ crucial	形 重要的	類 pivotal

併購

□ merger	名 合併	
□ buyout	名 收購	類 acquisition
□ cover	動 報導	類 report on

會計

□ budget	名 預算	
□ surplus	名 盈餘	類 black ink, in the black
□ profit	名 收益	類 earnings
□ deficit	名 赤字	類 red ink, in the red
□ income	名 收入	類 revenue
□ expense	名 支出	類 expenditure
□ debt	名 負債	類 borrowing

股票

□ stock	名 股份，股票	類 share	
□ shareholder	名 股東	類 stockholder	
□ investment	名 投資		
□ asset	名 資產		
□ capital	名 資本		

經濟

□ boost	動 提高，增加	類 increase	
□ soar	動 激增，暴漲		
□ boom	名 景氣繁榮	類 favorable business climate	
□ upsurge	名 急劇上升，高漲		
□ upturn	名 上升；好轉		
□ recession	名 不景氣，衰退	類 slump, depression, economic crisis	

其他

□ chief	形 主要的	類 primary	
□ authorize	動 授權，認可，允許	類 approve, consent to, grant permission	
□ cite	動 引用	類 quote	
□ meet	動 符合，滿足（一定條件）	類 fulfill, satisfy	
□ potential	形 潛在的	類 prospective	
□ void	形 無效的	類 invalid	

Day 10 模擬測驗
答案卡

Part 7

No.	ANSWER A B C D	No.	ANSWER A B C D	No.	ANSWER A B C D	No.	ANSWER A B C D	No.	ANSWER A B C D
1	Ⓐ Ⓑ Ⓒ Ⓓ	11	Ⓐ Ⓑ Ⓒ Ⓓ	21	Ⓐ Ⓑ Ⓒ Ⓓ	31	Ⓐ Ⓑ Ⓒ Ⓓ	41	Ⓐ Ⓑ Ⓒ Ⓓ
2	Ⓐ Ⓑ Ⓒ Ⓓ	12	Ⓐ Ⓑ Ⓒ Ⓓ	22	Ⓐ Ⓑ Ⓒ Ⓓ	32	Ⓐ Ⓑ Ⓒ Ⓓ	42	Ⓐ Ⓑ Ⓒ Ⓓ
3	Ⓐ Ⓑ Ⓒ Ⓓ	13	Ⓐ Ⓑ Ⓒ Ⓓ	23	Ⓐ Ⓑ Ⓒ Ⓓ	33	Ⓐ Ⓑ Ⓒ Ⓓ	43	Ⓐ Ⓑ Ⓒ Ⓓ
4	Ⓐ Ⓑ Ⓒ Ⓓ	14	Ⓐ Ⓑ Ⓒ Ⓓ	24	Ⓐ Ⓑ Ⓒ Ⓓ	34	Ⓐ Ⓑ Ⓒ Ⓓ	44	Ⓐ Ⓑ Ⓒ Ⓓ
5	Ⓐ Ⓑ Ⓒ Ⓓ	15	Ⓐ Ⓑ Ⓒ Ⓓ	25	Ⓐ Ⓑ Ⓒ Ⓓ	35	Ⓐ Ⓑ Ⓒ Ⓓ	45	Ⓐ Ⓑ Ⓒ Ⓓ
6	Ⓐ Ⓑ Ⓒ Ⓓ	16	Ⓐ Ⓑ Ⓒ Ⓓ	26	Ⓐ Ⓑ Ⓒ Ⓓ	36	Ⓐ Ⓑ Ⓒ Ⓓ	46	Ⓐ Ⓑ Ⓒ Ⓓ
7	Ⓐ Ⓑ Ⓒ Ⓓ	17	Ⓐ Ⓑ Ⓒ Ⓓ	27	Ⓐ Ⓑ Ⓒ Ⓓ	37	Ⓐ Ⓑ Ⓒ Ⓓ	47	Ⓐ Ⓑ Ⓒ Ⓓ
8	Ⓐ Ⓑ Ⓒ Ⓓ	18	Ⓐ Ⓑ Ⓒ Ⓓ	28	Ⓐ Ⓑ Ⓒ Ⓓ	38	Ⓐ Ⓑ Ⓒ Ⓓ	48	Ⓐ Ⓑ Ⓒ Ⓓ
9	Ⓐ Ⓑ Ⓒ Ⓓ	19	Ⓐ Ⓑ Ⓒ Ⓓ	29	Ⓐ Ⓑ Ⓒ Ⓓ	39	Ⓐ Ⓑ Ⓒ Ⓓ	49	Ⓐ Ⓑ Ⓒ Ⓓ
10	Ⓐ Ⓑ Ⓒ Ⓓ	20	Ⓐ Ⓑ Ⓒ Ⓓ	30	Ⓐ Ⓑ Ⓒ Ⓓ	40	Ⓐ Ⓑ Ⓒ Ⓓ	50	Ⓐ Ⓑ Ⓒ Ⓓ

No.	ANSWER A B C D
51	Ⓐ Ⓑ Ⓒ Ⓓ
52	Ⓐ Ⓑ Ⓒ Ⓓ
53	Ⓐ Ⓑ Ⓒ Ⓓ
54	Ⓐ Ⓑ Ⓒ Ⓓ

READING SECTION

國家圖書館出版品預行編目 (CIP) 資料

TOEIC® L&R TEST 多益閱讀解密 / Katsuno Shibayama、Robert Hilke、Paul Wadden 作;許可欣、黃薇嬪譯.
-- 初版. -- 臺北市:眾文圖書,民 107. 02 面;公分
ISBN 978-957-532-506-0(平裝) 1. 多益測驗
805.1895

106025169

TC031

TOEIC® L&R TEST 多益閱讀解密

定價 380 元

2018 年 10 月 初版 7 刷

作者	Katsuno Shibayama · Robert Hilke · Paul Wadden
譯者	許可欣 · 黃薇嬪
責任編輯	蔡易伶
總編輯	陳瑠琍
主編	黃炯睿
資深編輯	顏秀竹 · 蔡易伶
編輯	何秉修 · 黃婉瑩
美術設計	嚴國綸
行銷企劃	李皖萍
發行人	黃建和
發行所	眾文圖書股份有限公司
	台北市 10088 羅斯福路三段 100 號 12 樓之 2
網路書店	www.jwbooks.com.tw
電話	02-2311-8168
傳真	02-2311-9683
郵政劃撥	01048805

ISBN 978-957-532-506-0
Printed in Taiwan